CLEARING OF THE MIST

RICHARD F. FLECK

Dustbooks : Paradise : California : 1979

Published by Dustbooks,
P.O. Box 100, Paradise,
CA 95969

Clearing Of The Mist
is #10 in
The "American Dust" Series

ISBN 0-913218-86-3/cloth/$7.95
0-913218-85-5/paper/$2.95

Library of Congress Cataloging in Publication Data

Fleck, Richard

    Clearing of the mist.

    (The American dust series; no. 10)
    I. Title.
PZ4.F5862Cl [PS3556.L43]   813'.5'4   78-31884
ISBN 0-913218-86-3
ISBN 0-913218-87-1 pbk.

For my Irish wife, Maura, our children,
Rich, Michelle, Maureen,
and the children of Ireland

TABLE OF CONTENTS

CLEARING OF THE MIST

CHAPTER I
Slieve Gullion

Slanting sheets of cold grey rain drilled to the ground in darkening skies enveloping the slopes of Slieve Gullion in Northern Ireland. Two IRA fugitives, Steven and Michael, tramped over miles of spongy bogs in search of shelter. Green heather and dried out whinbush cracked in the wind while black swirls of crows whirled through the skies above rain-soaked potato fields lined with crowns of soft yellow ash trees and reddened hawthorn bushes.

"I'm after seein' a wee shed in a vale below," whispered Michael. *"Do ya s'pose we should check into it or not?"*

"With me drippin' wet and soaked through you ask such a question," replied Steven.

They picked up their pace and slid over a dark muddy rill down to an ancient stone shed. It was abandoned with cracked glass windows leaking badly but with some moldy piles of hay smelling as primeval as pre-Christian Ireland when wild Celts wandered through dense fern-filled rain forests. The two exhausted men put down their small weapons and ammunition and stretched out on the damp hay.

"Will ya listen to that wild wind," Michael implored.

"These days do weary a man; what with raidin' and runnin' from Fork Hill to here you might not give a bloody damn about livin' another day let alone worryin' about the wind, Michael."

1

In the distance an explosion reverberated through the grey misty valleys followed by some rifle fire which putted and patted like toy guns.

"Our boys is at it again. You know it's a pity them tommies spotted us. We'd still be with out lads," Steven remarked with vehemence. Michael just stared up at the cobwebs lacing the shed's rotting beams. A yellow moon peeped through storm clouds casting its sad, dim light on the floor. Michael got up to look out the window up at the misty summit of Slieve Gullion cropped with rocks as though the legendary giant Finn MacCool piled them there. He spotted the nearby ruins of an old household consisting of one stone wall and the slender remains of a chimney. His hand happened to touch something damp and covered with mildew just above the warped windowsill.

"Will ya look at this now," he said excitedly.

"What is it, Michael?"

"Looks like a bloody auld book or somethin'."

Michael opened it up to see that it was a barely legible diary written in the faint hand of Brian McBride and dated 1890.

Wonder who the devil Brian McBride was now," Michael said as he quickly leafed through the pages. He saw that the writing wasn't so badly frayed beyond the first few pages.

"Give me yer flashlight would ya, Steven."

They sat down looking at the nineteenth-century handwriting, and Michael began to read aloud.

"Oh God, it was hard times then. We all had great hunger. When was it now? Must have been forty or forty-five years ago over in Cavan." As Michael was reading, two British helicopters approached the damp green slopes of Slieve Gullion. The high pitched whirl of choppers' blades frightened the two IRA rebels who buried themselves in the hay. Spotlights from the choppers criss-crossed the floors and walls of the cowshed. A monkey puzzle tree's branches hissed violently outside in the artificial wind. Splotches of

2

rain hit the windows horizontally as though the planet's very orbit had changed. The only sound they could hear for endless minutes was a hypnotizing *whiss-whiss-whiss-whiss.*

"*When will those Prostestant bastards get out of here,*" whispered Steven.

"*Whist, will ya Steven.*"

After ten terrifying minutes, the choppers crept onward like grotesque, giant dragonflies toward the bald summit of the mountain, and dismal rain came pouring down from a dark cloud totally obscuring the pale whitening moon. Steven crawled out of the hay and sneaked out of the shed looking askance at the disappearing choppers. He walked past the ruins of the house to a trickling clear stream and laid down on its grassy bank for a drink. With all this rain you wouldn't think a man could develop a thirst, he thought to himself. As he ambled back, his eyes caught sight of a deserted church building without a cross in a lower vale and to its side were some tombstones which almost seemed to glow.

"*A bunch of dead Protestants,*" he mumbled. "*Better they are dead!*"

He trekked back up to the shed and found Michael looking at the diary with his flashlight as though nothing had ever happened.

"*Michael, for the love of God put out that light will ya.*"

"*Ah now, listen to this!*"

He continued reading aloud. "Both me parents looked like death itself. God, I hated to look into them sunken faces after they gave us children half their small plates of hot fried cabbage. I remember the rain leakin' in on us while we tried to sleep in that damp and cold thatched cottage. Me father was too weak to pick rushes for re-thatchin'. How long was it now before she died? God, I must have been only seventeen when it happened. Me mother developed a bad chest cough and spat blood. I think it was early winter or thereabouts. It was shockin' cold weather, and our turf bog was about all used up what with the neighbors and towns-people coming there to share our peat. Me father really was too weak to help much and me brother and sister were bloody small babes. I remember puttin' a hot water bottle at the feet of me mother and she saying it wasn't no use as she was going to her Creator anyway for she had heard a lone dog wailing that morning. Then it was that she vomited up blood and bile somethin' fierce. I just looked out at the dark skies streamin' with drops of icy rain cryin' to meself. I didn't even have the heart to tell me father she was dead with he lyin' in the next room so weak. I somehow managed to comfort me wee brother and sister.

Mother was a soft spoken woman. She seemed to accept her lot, though I don't know how. God, how she would love us children to death tellin' us stories and makin' us toys out of auld paper or straw. Before Gary was born she took Teresa and me to a hilltop covered with rushes and black-berry bushes. We could see clear to Northern Ireland even if it was misty and grey. How many times Teresa and I would return to that hill pretendin' mother was with us when she was really at home busy with chores. Me father loved her in his own way. He didn't do much talkin' wid her, but ya could tell there was love in his big brown eyes.

After we buried her in her cold, lonesome grave, me father never was the same, and how fast he failed, almost as fast as his potato crops. With his long grey beard he looked like Brian Boru himself only a dying Brian Boru. He said that's who I was named after."

Michael's eyes grew tired with a mere flashlight for illumination of the McBride diary.

"I think I'll have a wee look up the hill to see if the Tommies is gone yet, Steven."

"Mind ye, don't let 'em spot ya."

Michael stepped gingerly out of the dark shed and looked up at the shimmering moon casting silver clouds aglow. No helicopters were to be seen and all looked peaceful. He didn't even hear any distant rifle fire from the valley below.

Walking past some spiney hawthorne bushes and eating their red pithy berries, he spotted the abandoned Protestant church down the hill. Something drove him on toward that building which reflected glowing moonbeams. He soon found himself in the moldering graveyard looking at white tombstones sticking above the grasses like prehistoric bones. Then he saw it: "Brian McBride, 1830-1891."

"McBride, a Protestant!" he muttered.

Michael climbed up through the damp heather toward his companion at the cowshed determined to spend the rest of the evening reading the diary aloud. Safe from the British, he knew that McBride's life would be his for one starry night beneath the looming shadows of Slieve Gullion.

CHAPTER II

Death and Eviction

Me father always talked about Wolfe Tone when he was well. He said if Wolfe Tone had been listened to, we wouldn't be suffering the way we were. All Irishmen under Irish rule was his solution to overbearing absentee landlords and ridiculous rents. Look at our landlord, the Earl of Chapwick. He expected me father to pay ten pounds an acre rental. The Earl must have had a hundred of us doing the same while he sat back in England eating his stuffed goose washed down with fine French wines. Now what right did that bloody Englishman have to Irish lands to begin with?

God, I remember me wee sister Teresa followed by our dog Patch comin' back home with her skirts full of juicy blackberries and green nettles while we was diggin' spuds out in the fields. We was to put aside so much spuds and barley to pay rent for our land, and them blackberries stopped us from eatin' too much of our profits. Profits, that's a laugh! You might think we was bloody Capitalists or somethin'. When angry auld Derid Joyce came by to col- lect our grain and spuds for Chapwick, he wasn't no gentle- man I tell ya.

"Fill up me wagons fast now would ya," he'd say. "I ain't got all day to wait ya know. I have to collect from ten more cultchies* down the road and then go into town to sell what I can."

When was it now? Somewhere around October of 1846 a few bleak weeks before me father died. Father felt well enough to go out in the rain with me to dig a few muddy drills of spuds for storage.

"What's this," he said.

---

* Farmfolk

7

God, when I looked into the drill, I saw a bunch of black, foul smellin' stuff that wasn't no potatoes I'll tell ya. One of our neighbors, James Harris, I think it was, said we should put our wash out over the drills and them spuds would be alright. Well we didn't have all that much wash to spread over the muddy auld fields, but it worked, by God! We'd dig them drills and put away some good potatoes I'll tell ya. But most of our crop was rotten, and our rent was in grave jeopardy.

That month it rained and rained. The hills of Cavan looked grey, and each cottage always seemed to have a wee curl of peat smoke comin' out of its stark chimney to kill the damp chill about the house. Our whitewashed walls dampened with layers of water oozing out of them on the inside and out. Our auld pictures of Dublin City hanging in the sitting room were ruined. We received some sort of notice from a stuffy auld county official that we couldn't read but which our minister read for us telling us we should sprinkle a lime solution or somethin' over earth-covered potatoes. Now where in the world would we get that much lime for five acres of spuds? It's no wonder me father started to fail. And when he heard news from Mr. Harris, his health failed all the more.

"The whole ground is poisoned," James Harris exclaimed.

"What do ya mean, James," questioned Edward McBride from his mat.

"Just that! Swirls of crows wouldn't light on me fields because they're poisoned. I went up to me north brey, up past them rows of blackberries your daughter goes to, and started diggin'. Some Catholic lads were helpin' with the harvest, and ya know we filled up four brave wagonloads with healthy enough lookin' spuds. Lough Gowna just glowed in the sunny mist far off, and we was all feelin' pretty spry I'll tell ya."

"Ya still haven't told me what ya mean yer ground is poisoned!"

"We took them wagonloads down to the barn and piled

'em up in storage while the old chestnut brown horses wheezed in the damp air outside with puffs of steam comin' out of their nostrils. By God, in just three or four days them potatoes rotted into a black mass! It has to be the bloody ground itself. There must be a cure for the ground." He looked down to the floor of the McBride cottage fearing the strange look he would get from the sick man.

"James. Remember you told me to put out wash over the drills. That worked! We got about a hundred stone of foine potatoes yer welcome to share."

"Look here, Edward. I tried it meself, and it didn't work!"

"Well go and look at me spuds and see fer yerself."

Harris took leave of his old companion and went out to the barn where I was busy milking a cow. Piles of rich brown spuds lay there waiting to be eaten.

"Yer father is right. You had luck puttin' clothes over yer potato drills."

"That's what you told us to do Mr. Harris."

"Aye, but it didn't work for me after I told yous."

"God, do ya think these here spuds is alright, then?"

I grabbed a big potato and broke it open to see its white and fresh smelling inside. They seemed alright to me. I even bit into one, and it tasted normal.

"Get yerself a sack and fill it up would ya."

"Well if ya don't mind, but I'll bring over a fresh turkey fer yous."

"Ya needn't bother with that, now."

"Indeed, I will!"

We walked back to me father's foul smelling room and told him all was well, and he smiled for the first time since mother had died. He told me to care for our wee babe Gary who was cryin' somethin' fierce. Without his mother Gary had become a bit of a problem. Teresa was no real help except for gathering blackberries for fruit and nettles for soup; I was always stinging meself with nettles. I didn't know rightly how to fold the leaves.

I gave Gary his porridge and took a wee ramble with Teresa up the brey. God, there was a chill in the air with them grey clouds hugging the wet fields and shooks.* We picked some haws from the ever-rustling hawthorn bushes and spat out the pits as it started to rain. Grey sheets of rain is what gives Ireland its forty shades of green they say.

"Brian, please don't let's talk of mommy; I couldn't stand it."

"Of course we won't, Teresa."

"Brian, what are we goin' to do when them spuds is eaten up?"

"We'll put more wash out on the drills."

"But didn't Mr. Harris say it wasn't working no more?"

"Aye, but we'll see. I can catch us some good trout in Lough Gowna for by** if it comes to that."

"Aye, I s'pose you could."

We ambled back to our cottage and put on some tea. Father was coughing awful bad in the back room. He sounded like one of them steam engines ya hear in the cities. Teresa wet the tea, and we brought a hot and steaming cupper to father.

"Daddy, what are we gonna do when them spuds is all gone?"

"Teresa, will ya whist," I shouted.

"Ya know, Brian," me father said in a rasping voice. "Wolfe Tone was a brave man, a brave man indeed." He took a deep and noisy swill of tea. "Yes, Tone went to the French for help just about fifty years ago when I was your age."

"Was he Catholic father?"

"Ah no, Protestant. A Protestant who fought against the British but lost."

"What happened to him?"

---

* ditches.
**besides.

10

"He took his own life, and when he did, so did Ireland."

"Will ya look out the window, father. Me gory if it isn't snowin'."

Father just quivered a little and began that horrible coughing again. It was about that time that Derid Joyce came knocking at the door demanding his portion of spuds and grain for rent. I told him we hadn't got but a hundred stone of potatoes and a few hundred weight of barley. That would do rightly he said. When I asked what would we be eating, he simply shrugged his shoulders and said that's your problem now, isn't it? He clutched a turkey from Harrises that was meant for us.

"Give the man what he wants," father shouted in a deep and melancholic tone. "And you'd better let Patch fair for himself—he's a smart enough dog." Joyce and his helper loaded up the wagon with our food. I managed to put aside five good stone of spuds in a dark corner. I hadn't ever seen it snow so fiercely before. I missed me mother something fierce. She'd be so cheerful in weather like this telling us of our granda who was a school teacher knowing how to read and write. We still had some of his books lyin' about in the house or cowshed gathering mold and mildew. I liked to look at the pictures of all them grey bearded leaders, though I didn't know who they were. Maybe me father got all that talk of Wolfe Tone from granda. Perhaps we had one of Tone's books, and I didn't even know it.

After a week of heavy blowing snows our spuds was gone and so was our barley. It was too cold to go fishing—Lough Gowna was frozen I think, and we didn't even have nettles or weeds. Father called me with faint voice into the room while I was tryin' to give wee Gary a sup a tea.

"Joyce will come again, and when he does he'll force us out."

"I know, father, but the Harris's will be out too."

"They'll be takin' only me body out, son."

"Ah, hush, now. You'll be livin' longer than me."

"You'll have to get someone to care for Gary and Teresa. And you, me son, must go to .. America . . . "

"I'd take them with me if I could find the money."

A few days later Edward McBride coughed his last cough and passed away. I think his last word was "America." Just a wee trickle of blood came out of the corner of his mouth. Teresa came into the room. She knew what had happened before I had a chance to speak.

"Not Daddy dead! Isn't Mommy enough! Oh Brian, what in heavens name will we do? It appears God ain't willin' to help us. What will we do?"

Just then our dog Patch snarled and growled. He hadn't eaten in weeks. We backed away and out of the room. It is too terrible to even think about it. We heard the sounds of tearing and chewing and gnawing. My God, me own father was being eaten up by Patch! I ran out of the miserable house and down the brey to Reverend Samuel's home to call for help. When he entered father's room all that we could hear was "Oh my God!" He wouldn't let us in the room and told me to go find Patch. I found him in the whinbushes by our old trash heap and dragged him home by the collar, he whimpering all the while. Reverend Samuel, that same peaceful man who spoke so calmly of a loving God each Sunday in our little country church, smashed his horrid skull in with a mighty big rock from the lane and threw Patch's body into the trash heap. I helped him carry the remains of me father's body in a blanket, while Teresa cared for Gary who never stopped cryin' and naggin' for food. When we buried father in a shallow, snowy grave, Reverend Samuel said a few words from Ephesians; I think it was "Grace be to you and peace from God our Father, and from the Lord Jesus Christ." I thought the word "grace" was a bit too ridiculous for referring to a cold body all chewed up. I only saw his one hand dropping from inside the blanket. It had only two frozen fingers left.

We three children cried all night at Reverend Samuel's place, and the next day he told us to go fetch our belongings. When Teresa and I got there, none other than Mr. Joyce was waitin' and demanded his "fair" share of spuds. When I told him what happened he said "you'll not step into claim any belongings; I'll be takin' them for security. Yous is all evicted, and this property belongs to the Earl of Chapwick. Now get, will yous!" He chased us with a stick.

When Teresa and I ran back to our minister's house, he said there was nothing he could do for us, but he'd see to it that Gary would be cared for by someone better off than we. Since I was seventeen, I'd have to care for Teresa who was six by finding work on the roads—how and where was me own problem.

CHAPTER III

Living in a Ditch

Hard weeks had passed, and Teresa and I lived with the Harrises in a deep old ditch on the Monaghan border. They, too, had been evicted. Some auld potato sacks served as our roof supported by spiney hawthorn sticks. We had caught some glistening wet frogs in a nearby icy bog and were roasting them over an open fire. There must have been six inches of snow on the ground that grey November. Mr. Harris said in all his life he had never seen so much snow. It wasn't the snow that was so bad as not having decent shoes or over-clothes to go out into it. But living in that ditch proved to be, I won't say happy, but a wee joyful compared to the hell we'd been through. Every stranger that came trampin' by stopped to stay with us a while. We all shared what we had even if it was worms or raw cabbage or dried up haws. We'd hear stories of the good times in Ireland. I remember one wee elf of a man talking:

"About a year or so ago, I got a pot of the best damned spuds in the land boilin' with a plate of creamy butter just in the waitin'. I had been quite drunk ya know and was lookin' forward to fillin' me poor stomach with somethin' appetizing. Well, I took a wee nap waitin' for the spuds to boil, and the next thing ya know I smell somethin' borning. I gets up off the floor and rushes over to me hearth to find a pot of burnt and smoking remains of them good spuds." We all did a bit of laughing at that until we felt a yearning for spuds. Oh, for a good auld spud instead of cabbage leaves and more cabbage leaves! We all looked pretty thin I'll tell ya. You could pull the skin away from our arms and legs like skin from a rotten tomato.

One day a young Roman Catholic priest came by to tell us they was givin' out something called Indian corn in the town of Cavan, and it would be worth our goin' for it. I was elected to make the journey some ten miles distant. It wasn't too long before I felt a good bit tired what with not eatin' proper. As I passed the farm gates of an old cabin, a young woman dressed in black waved to me and started shoutin'.

"Young man, lend me a hand, would ya?"

"I'm going for food and can't."

"It will only take a few minutes."

"What is it ya want?"

"To help bury me husband."

I don't know why, but I walked up the path of frozen mud to her cabin. Inside there was a stench something frightful. Then I saw a body wrapped up in a soggy blanket. We dragged him across the planks of the floor with her sobbing all the while. She was a beautiful woman with long black hair and soft brown eyes. I dug a hole through the snow with an old loy* into the frozen ground. All I could do was bury him in the snow and put rocks over the corpse.

"He's been dead near a week now."

"Why didn't you get someone to bury him before this?"

"I was too upset. He couldn't even get me pregnant, ya know."

As she was talking she bared her white breasts and asked me to come with her into her room. Me bein' only seventeen, I was frightened out of me life. I told her to her face while she slipped out of her ragged old dress showin' me everything she had that I would do no such thing. I had to get food for me family who was starvin' in a ditch.

"I'm starvin' too, ya know."

"Why do you want to be pregnant in these horrible times?"

"It's not being pregnant I want—it's getting pregnant."

Her breasts hung low and curved up again. It was all I could

---

* shovel

16

do to leave her and that stenchy room. She had a lovely body with long white legs. But I left her to her misery. I had misery enough. All the way to Cavan I kept thinkin' of them two breasts and her long black hair at her shoulders. I tramped for miles on end with two frozen blocks for feet. Skies grew darker and darker. God, it was a good sight to see the town of Cavan with warm peat smoke risin' from all the chimneys.

I entered a dingy supply station set up by the "merciful" British for distributing Indian corn. One old man sitting in a chair was saying, "Tis an irony that our potato blight came from North America to begin with, and now they want us to eat American corn meal." I grabbed a one stone sack and was told how to cook the miserable looking grub. The same old man asked me to sit down and share a bottle of porter he had tucked away. Another couple of blokes were singing to some fiddle music. It was the first singing I heard in over a year when me father and me would go into town to sell sucker pigs.

"Tell me lad, now that you've had a taste of porter, how yous is fairing out in the country."

"How do you know I'm from the country?"

"Ya ain't from Cavan, I'll tell ya."

"Aye, I'm from the country alright, and me father and mother are after being buried in shallow graves. Me and me sister is livin' in a ditch with another family."

"Is this yer first corn meal?"

"Aye, I'm not lookin' forward to it, though I'm fairly well famished."

"See that banner up there on the wall. It says 'Simpler the needs, simpler the wants'. If your needs are simple you'll tolerate it lad. But if I was as young as you, I'd think about leavin' for America."

"That's what me father told me, too."

"A man can get to Canada, they say, for three or four pound."

"Three or four pound may as well be a sovereign—I

17

ain't got no such money!"

"A foine young lad the likes of you could get work on the roads, ya know."

"For what wages?"

"'Bout six pence a day."

"It would be many days work before I'd save enough for America."

"Aye, but think of it lad."

"Ah sure, I can't leave me wee sister."

"What age has she?"

"Six or seven years."

"Then you have a problem, man."

"Aye," I said as I got up to walk back to me ditch home with the sack of meal. It started snowing hard and me toes was about frozen by the time I reached that house with the naked lady. I thought I heard her sobbing but I didn't dare go in. The wind blew something fierce, and you know I couldn't find our miserable ditch hut? I looked in the blinding snow with me wet bag of Indian corn and couldn't find the bloody shelter. Where in heaven's name was Teresa and the Harrises?

I must have gone too far and just didn't see them with the wind blowing all that blinding snow. God that Indian corn was gettin' heavy. As I backtracked along the lonely road between the frozen hedgerows and naked hawthorn branches, I heard some whimpering in the distance. I scampered along past snow-laden ash trees covered with brown, withered ivy up to our ditch hut.

"Thank God you're back," Mr. Harris said. "Somethin's wrong with our baby. It must be the famine fever. He's burning hot and broken out in rashes."

"Mr. Harris, I got some Indian corn here. We'll boil it up in no time and feed the poor wee thing as well as ourselves."

We put a couple handfuls of ground meal into a boiling kettle and stirred for several minutes and then scooped some into auld cracked china bowls. Teresa just smiled and ate her bowl full while Mrs. Harris fed the wee babe. I thought the meal was terrible stuff and forced it down. It was hard and gritty with a shockin' bad flavor. So this was our gift from the British! Later that evening the Harris' baby just kept cryin' and moaning with a bloated stomach. The snow was falling down and blowing into our ditch with a terrible force. We was all shivering and feeling bleak inside like there never was good times in Ireland.

"We've got to get the cure for this child," Mr. Harris grumbled. "I wonder if Hugh McFarland is still about. He used to give the cure for near any ailment on this here earth."

"Do ya want me to go look for him," says I.

"Ah no, I'll go meself with the first morning's light."

"Well, I'll get up and put some twigs on the fire anyway."

"Aye, perhaps we could have more of the Indian meal."

"If you want, I'll put some on in a jiffy."

After Mr. Harris and I had some painful spoonfulls of what tasted like water and gritty auld sawdust, we tried to feed the wee suffering babe, but it would just vomit the corn meal and scream and wail. No one got any sleep that night with the shockin' cold winds and the wailing noise of the baby.

Faint glimmers of pink threaded the pale winter sky as Mr. Harris left in search of Hugh McFarland. The day came clear and a bit more mild with the December sun rising above old stooks of brown hay pushing above the crusty snow. The distant green hills of Monaghan even seemed to have mist or haze risin' from them like the steam from our breaths. In a few hours we heard tramping feet.

"Sarah," Mr. Harris shouted to his wife, "Here's Hugh McFarland. He's got a cure, I'm sure for our baby."

They both trudged into the ditch, McFarland wearing his black Wellingtons and an auld grey coat. He was a funny looking man with a stubbly grey beard and bloodshot duck eyes. Bangs of grey hair covered his forehead.

"Let's see the babe," he said.

"Aye, here it is. He's all covered with a rash and burning with the fever. He can't hold anything down and is loose at both ends."

"Aye, we'll just put some of these here critters on him for a wee while." McFarland took from a pouch two ugly black leeches and put them on the arms of the Harris child. Blood immediately trickled down its white, soft flesh. The curer made some weird gestures and danced a jug mumbling strange gypsy-sounding words.

"Now listen. Wrap the wee fellow in blankets and follow me. We all walked a mile or so down the lane past the breasty woman's house to a tree with a mighty cleft in it. I think it was a old chestnut tree. McFarland stood on one side of the cleft and Mr. Harris on the other.

"Now hand me the child through the tree."

"Aye, but what will this do?"

"T'will pass his sickness into the tree and he'll live to a brave age."

"Oh, aye, oh God, aye."

Strangely enough the baby did seem to quiet down, but them leeches on his arms made me sick. Sarah Harris felt the babe's forehead, and the fever did seem lower. Well, all we could do was give Hugh McFarland one stone of corn meal which he refused. Then Mr. Harris went to his trunk in the back of the ditch and offered him an old picture of leprechauns on the misty summit of Ben Bulbas. McFarland grasped the picture with drunken glee as it must have had some magic in it. That evening we sat about our fire warming our frozen hands.

"If we'd only had a wee trout to fry," said I. "I remember fishin' in Lough Gowna just last spring standin' on a pebbly bank lined with leafy chestnut trees beset with glowing patches of shamrocks. Why I'd just throw out me line with a worm on the end of it and before long me hook would be janglin' with a firm trout! It was so peaceful there watchin' swans drift by and corncrakes flutter in nearby green fields."

"Them days is gone forever, lad," reflected Mr. Harris.

"Aye, it's more than days that is gone—our pride, too, Mr. Harris. Here we are eating the bait that we used to fish with!"

"Aye," Harris groaned, "Aye. We shoulda followed our neighbors Johnny and Mary Fields to America. Maybe our babe wouldn't a become so sick. Maybe we'd be eatin' a square meal."

"Perhaps," I said quietly.

Christmas must have come and gone without our knowing it as we didn't know one day from the next, nor did we have much joy to share except in the baby's seeming recovery. As I later learned, the Harris child probably had typhus fever, and it was in the remission stage when Teresa and I decided to go off to Dublin all on our own. Probably the wee babe died; I never did find out, as when I came back to Ireland no record existed of the Harrises. Before we left for the bleak sixty mile trek to Dublin, we checked with Reverend Samuel to find out he didn't even remember where Gary was sent. Maybe he was dead, but we left him in God's hands.

Teresa and I had a long, cold, and tiring walk to Dublin. It took us some five days as we were weak and had to stop at food dispensaries wherever we heard tell of them. All that I remember is miles and miles of cold, sleety hills with a few patches of green and lines on end of leafless trees lining misty breys. Not a cow, chicken, sheep or goat was to be seen anywhere. Most of the bleak old homes looked deserted with no smoke comin' out of the chimneys. Fresh graves spotted the fields here and there with make-shift crosses. I never remember Ireland as being so desolate and hellish, but those are the only words fit to describe her. Teresa asked me why God would permit such suffering and terror. All I could say was God must be English. We walked and talked for miles on end until we thought we saw something in the far distance. Ah sure it was a foine good sight to see black plumes of coal smoke risin' above Dublin town!

CHAPTER IV

Soup Kitchens of Dublin

Teresa asked me to get her some warm food and drink now that we reached the paved streets of Dublin with rows of brick homes, copper domed buildings and grand bridges over the River Liffey. I saw a man munching on some dried auld seaweed and asked him where he got it. Teresa and I followed his rambling directions to the shoreline, and sure enough we saw the rocks he mentioned. But when I approached the rocks what did I see but a guard of women with clubs standin' around. They told me to get my fecking body out of here if I knew what was good and that any seaweeds or snails belonged to their neighborhood and no stranger's. They said to try Soyer's Soup Kitchen; we'd surely get food there. Well we was half starved with the hunger walkin' all them grey pavements past grey auld buildings and sooty monuments and past ragged beggars and blind men and women askin' the same sort of questions of me that that widow did back in Cavan. Finally we saw a long line of shabby looking people waitin' to go into Soyer's Soup Kitchen. One hundred of us entered a dark and narrow passage way, and we were told to wait for the sound of a bell. A tall, distinguished, grey-haired lady with a matronly voice was with us waiting for the bell. She looked at me and Teresa and asked,

"What part of the country are you from?"

"Cavan," we said shyly.

"Cavan is a distinctly rural sector of our beleagured nation, and you must be representative peasants. I am from Belfast, you see. What the problem is here as we all can tell is that we have all fallen out of favor with the Lord." Someone in the crowd asked her to shut her gob, but she just rambled on.

23

"I can see that you undeserving peasants are waiting for a handout here in Dublin when you have no right to be here. You are probably Catholics aren't you? They don't allow Catholics here."

"No, we ain't mame," I said, "didn't you say you was from Belfast?"

"I said no such thing. I originated in Belfast but am a current resident of Dublin and *have* spoken with the Lord, and I shall act for the Lord by denying you undeserving wretches *our* soup."

"Shut yer gob," several of the shivering crowd shouted.

"The Lord giveth and the Lord taketh, and you miserable wretches should have been taken. *I* know that I speak with authority. When I was sewing this morning, I knew that each stitch I made was life given to one of you, but if I unstitch, where are you?"

"Shut yer gob."

"I say that I know for I am the way, and I shall be given one of your bowls of soup as I . . . "

"Shut yer gob!"

"I need the soup more than any of you wretches and vermin with typhus and other diseases. Why did I not un-stitch what I have stitched?"

A red faced, gaunt man came up to her and punched her in the face. Blood spurted out of her nose as she blurted out,

"The Lord shall . . . " and she was hit again and pushed into the alley. Just then a clanging bell rang, and we all pushed and shoved toe to heel into a dreary dark room lined with white bowls filled with steaming soup with a wee slice of dark bread. We were told to commence eating, and we all slurped away. God it was good to get somethin' hot in our weary stomachs. Teresa politely asked for a second helping but her bowl was taken away, rinsed and returned empty. When we were all finished after five minutes or so our bowls were rinsed and reset. A policeman rang that irritating, grating bell as we were herded out, and a new

24

hungry crowd entered.

"Brian, let's get in line again! I don't care if we run into that crazy woman again."

Before I had a chance to answer her, another policeman shouted at Teresa,

"Ah no ya don't! Try it and see what happens. We check faces ya know."

I told the policeman that we weren't Catholics, but he said it didn't matter. Then I asked him where I might find work. He said to try the railway station three blocks down the street but not to expect anything.

"Come on, Teresa, let's go."

"Aye, I will, but I'm still a good bit hungry ya know."

"There'll be more soup tomorrow."

"I don't think I can wait till then."

"Aye, ya will indeed."

We walked along the main street of Dublin whose name I didn't know as I couldn't read and past a number of well lit pubs with some men drinking dark porter. I stopped to ask what a glass of porter cost and was told one and a half pence. I hadn't had porter since getting Indian corn at Cavan. Me father used to like his porter. Every Friday, we'd go into town to sell our crops or livestock for to buy food we couldn't grow, and he and I would stop off at McCardles for a tall pint glass of porter. God, it was good stuff, ya know. To think me poor father's mutilated body lies rotting in a shallow grave! Where in God's name was Gary? The whole world was turned upside down; everything seemed so distant like it was a dream. I grabbed Teresa to hold her close to me as we walked toward the railway station past dark alleys where hungry hounds barked. God, I remember the lonely sounds of Patch barking in the bogs on foggy mornings like he was some kind of hound of hell. I'd a killed him then had I only known. But we're prisoners of time. Time has teeth like no mere hound.

We climbed some fierce steps up to the grey building filled with the sound of screaming locomotive whistles and hissing steam. I soon found the head man to ask about work and was pleased to hear that a railway line was being built from Dublin to Cork, and they needed lots of able men to help lay ties and track. I was told to report to work the next morning for eight pence a day. There's pay for ya! With eight pence I could buy some porter, some foine new clothing for me and Teresa and maybe even . . . But, wait, I asked him where would I live? He told me in the worker's quarters. When I inquired where my sister would stay he said he hadn't the foggiest. Didn't I have no relatives in Dublin he asked. You know, I wasn't sure but maybe me father's unmarried sister worked somewhere in Dublin.

"Aye," Teresa recalled. "Doesn't our Aunt Sissy work for some butcher here in Dublin?"

The railroad man asked what our last name was and when he heard "McBride," he asked, "Are yous Protestants?"

"Aye, we are."

"All I know is there are a lot of Protestant McBrides on Baggott Street."

"Aye," Teresa said. "It was Baggott Street I think where the butcher shop was."

"How do you remember somethin' like that, Teresa?"

"Because Auntie Sissy said Baggott Street."

"But how do you remember it was Baggott Street?"

"Because Baggott rhymes with maggott, and she said maggots were the curse of a butcher."

Snow had changed to rain, and the streets of Dublin were slick with ice. Me sister and I walked toward a lonely auld part which I think was called Saint Stephen's Green on the other side of the grey Liffey which flowed quietly and softly with a few scrawny gulls flying about. We entered the park with brilliantly green exposed patches of grass almost too painful to look at. The tall grey buildings lurched above the trees while pigeons fluttered from ice heap to dirty auld ice heap. We shivered with the damp and cold hoping somebody might come by who would tell us where Baggott Street was. A few half naked beggar women came by asking for ha' pennies which we didn't have. A horse and carriage clip clopped down the cold cobblestone street nearby 'with trailing echoes between the red brick buildings and grey stone monuments. The air was so heavy in Dublin! A young lad with his mother came by, at last and they obligingly told us where Baggott Street was.

"Teresa, you walk down the one side, and I'll walk on the other to look for that butcher shop."

"Aye, a clever idea."

Well, I'll tell ya now—it was a good three hours of trampin' the wet streets and askin' ten different butcher shops if a Sissy McBride worked there. In the dark misty hours of evening, one butcher said that Sissy McBride was dead of fever over a fortnight ago but that her cousin worked in a linen mill at Rathmines. We both trudged back to Saint Stephen's Green and stretched out on a frozen bench to try and sleep. But the cold was fierce. Rain changed to snow, and winds blew constantly all night long. Me shoes was open at the toes, and Teresa's shoes were badly warped and damp, but somehow we managed to sleep an hour or two in what proved to be the longest night I had ever spent in Ireland. I was half tempted to go across the green to a fancy British hotel where somebody like the Earl of Chapwick may have visited when he checked on how Derid Joyce and others were doing for him, but there was too many policemen about, and surely they would have kicked us out. How could a man eat Dublin prawn while others contented themselves with rotten cabbage leaves? Some lucky few men must have still believed in Reverend Samuel's "kind God."

By early dawn, we dragged our stiff bones to Soyer's Soup Kitchen and waited in line in the back alley. Rats were scampering here and there, but we paid no mind as our stomachs were scampering too. God, it was good to hear them bells clanging away to let the first group in. Then came our turn to enter that dingy, warm hall. We slurped our luke warm soup and ate a wee slice of bread, but poor Teresa found a mouse's tail in her soup and had to run out and vomit on the street. I felt sorry for the wee girl. What hell she had been through! I told her things would be better once we found Aunt Sissy's cousin at Rathmines, but she would have to wait in the railway station all day while I worked.

Me boss told me I was ten minutes late, and one more time like that and I'd be out of work. I hopped on a flat car with twenty others and left grey auld Dublin behind as we sped southward toward the grey-green Dublin Mountains. God, it was bloody cold out there on that flat car. Me fingers about froze and me toes never did thaw out from the night before.

"Where ya from, lad?" asked an old hairlipped man.

"From County Cavan."

"Oh aye, I'm from Monaghan."

"What's this work like, me good man?"

"A good bit difficult. Lots of liftin' to do."

"Liftin what?"

"Ties to lay rails on."

On a devilishly lonely patch of field we stopped, and we were told to get out and go to a large pile of black ties. Hundreds of men were picking and shoveling off in the distance while our group picked up frosty ties and laid them astride each other about every three feet. A mile or so behind us an iron crew laid the rails on the ties and hammered them in place with big spikes. I don't know which was worse, diggin' spuds or layin' ties. Both were hard on me back. By the end of two hours or so I thought me kidneys were going to burst so I left the line for the leafless bushes below. Well, as I buttoned up me fork*, me eyes caught two skeletons face up in the mud. Them empty sockets and bare white teeth seemed to stare at me sayin' to leave this cursed land! Then I remembered me father's words about goin' to America as well as the old man from Cavan where I got the Indian

---

* flies

28

corn. I wondered what ever became of the naked lady near our ditch hut. It's funny how the mind wanders when yer living in a nightmare.

"Hurry up, man!" someone shouted from above.

"Aye, I am, but I'm after seein' two skeletons."

"Ah, come now, who in hell hasn't seen a skeleton or two. All of bloody Ireland is full of them. We're buildin' a railway for the dead!"

When I reached the work, I saw it was me foreman I was talkin' to.

"Get to woirk, now. Earn yer eight pence!"

We all worked till dark getting a cup of tea and a biscuit during the mid-day break. It was then I met an interesting school teacher turned laborer. We chatted from time to time. I remember Peter Flanigan, the teacher, told me with his breath showing in the cold, how he never thought much of whipping schoolboys, but he had to do it or he'd lose his job. He thought *because* he whipped them, God punished him by having him lose his job. Earth and heaven were against him. I was glad I met this man for I knew we'd be good friends. Traveling back on the flat car to Dublin was cold, bleak and wearisome. All I could think of was wee Teresa and how she would be waitin' for me at the station. Well I was in for a surprise, I'll tell ya. Teresa was standin' there with a young woman by the name of Elish McBride!

"Brian, Brian, I found our cousin!"

"Teresa, how in heaven's name did ya do it?"

"I asked where Rathmines was and found the old linen mill. It wasn't long till Elish came to see who it was that wanted her."

"Sure I'm happy you done that, Teresa."

Elish came up to me to offer her hand and welcome me.

"Pleased to make yer acquaintance, Brian."

"So am I pleased to make yours."

"Would yous come to me loft for a wee spread of tea,

biscuits and cheese?"

"Cheese, did you say? Aye, indeed we will; I have no great urge to go to Soyer's Soup again!"

We arrived after darkness at her flat which she shared with her step mother. There were several shelves of books in the sitting room so I knew me cousin, unlike we country folk, could read. She wasn't pulled out of school to work in the fields like me. While the step mother (Elish was probably her bastard daughter) didn't say much, Elish was the perfect host. Oh that cheese! It melted in me mouth, and I sort of let it slide slowly down me throat. To think there were no grits in it to scratch their way down to your stomach like that damnable Indian corn!

"Would you care for a wee glass of porter, Brian?"

"Oh God aye!"

I took long, slow swallows. This time I tasted it. Back at Cavan I was too worried to sense any flavor. Oh how it brought everythin' back.

On that first Sunday of every August we would hitch up a team of horses and all of us would go to Black Rock on the Monaghan line. We'd take off our shoes and Mother and Dad would lead the way over the dark sands speckled with broken clam and scallop shells. It was grand to watch the sea-weed spread out under each incoming wave like a girl's hair in a washtub. And auld Slieve Gullion rose up in the distance like some ghost out of the sea. Hundreds of gulls flew about laughin' like bloody humans. Then we'd all walk up to Finnigan's pub, and Dad and me would order a glass of porter. Mother and Teresa would sit in the lady's glassed-in room and look over the sea shells they had collected.

"So yer workin' with the railway, are ya?"

"Aye, for eight pence a day, it ain't bad."

"Sure it isn't. I'm gettin' but seven at the mill, and I've been there two years now ever since I finished school."

I got to looking at a musty auld print of Dublin on the wall. By George if it wasn't like the one in our old Cavan home.

God, how the mind drifts in times like these. Sammy Harris, Harris' grandfather, came into our foine thatched cottage when me father and mother were well and alive. He'd pull a flute out of his vest pocket and we'd start singing auld ballads while we all sat near the hearth cracklin' with peat embers. That was before Gary was born and the potato blight. Mother never was the same in health after Gary was born. But old Sammy Harris would play the flute lookin' somethin' like an auld leprechaun. Mother would wet the tea and fix a spread of spuds, trout, and fried cabbage. We didn't have all that much, but sure it was enough. Now mother is dead of some rotten disease and father lies mangled in the grave. God knows where Gary is, maybe back with his mother. Aye, it's just Teresa and me now, and she looks like she has found a new home, thank God.

"Have some more cheese, Brian."

"Ah, I'd better not, or I'll get too spoilt."

"Will ya stay with us tonight?"

"Ah no, mame. I have to stay in the worker's huts so as we can leave early in the morn."

"Well, anyway, you know Teresa is more than welcome to stay with us now."

"Tis a blessing, Elish, a blessing after so many curses!"

"You aren't leavin' already, Brian," Teresa questioned.

"Aye, sis. Here ya are wee girl—four pence of me eight. Take care, and I'd best be gettin' back as it's after dark."

"We'll see you tomorrow, Brian," remarked the step mother finally breaking her silence.

"Aye, I'll try."

Well, I'll tell ya, it was some few ragged weeks before I got back. Aye, it must have been March or sometime when mild weather finally returned after what seemed years of cold work south of Dublin liftin' ties, shovelin' gravel, and hammerin' cold spikes. God, it was hard work. Day in and day out of hammerin' and hammerin' and liftin'. I just didn't have the strength to walk out to Rathmines every day. I got used to Soyer's Soup Kitchen and salivated when the bell rang like some auld dog. But would you believe that I had over three pounds saved? Some railroad workers talked about British ships goin' over to Quebec, North America out of Cork for just three pound. The British ships gave you seven pounds of food a week for free so long as ya promised to settle in Canada and not America, though for some strange reason I always thought Canada was America. When I did go to Elish's, I didn't want to let on to Teresa I was leavin' until I was ready for tellin' her. I gave her two shillings to buy some warm clothes.

The two IRA rebels, Steven and Michael, heard a strange noise outside the cowshed.

"What's that, Michael?"

"God, I hope it ain't the British."

"I'll go have a look. Put out the bloody auld flashlight, will ya!"

Steven peaked out of the doorway and saw a wee goat nosing around the bushes outside the shed while the moon beamed down the silvery slopes of Slieve Gullion.

"Ah, sure, it's only a goat, Michael. Ya know, I'm a bit sleepy. It's nearly two in the morning, and we've got to get back to our boys tomorrow."

"Do as you please, Steven, but I'm gonna continue reading."

"Ah, but Michael, how am I gonna hear the rest of it. I wanna see if that poor bastard gets over to America or not."

"Canada, you mean."

"Aye."

"Well, I'll fill ya in on what happens when ya wake up in the morning, okay?"

"Aye."

Michael read through the hours of a dark, windy night. As early morning reddened the valleys below, British choppers flew all over.

"We'd best hide here a while longer, Steven."

"Aye, I think you're right. But for Lord's sake did Brian make it to America?"

"Brian, you mean Brian Campbell the footballer?"

"Ah no, Brian McBride, the bloody Protestant."

"Oh aye, aye, he made it all the way to the Dakota Territory."

"Fill me in will ya?"

"Well, where did ya leave off?"

"In Dublin about to tell Teresa he's leavin'."

"Did ya hear tell of the school teacher he met on the railroad gang?"

"Maybe, but I can't remember too well."

A few weeks before Brian returned to Rathmines to tell his sister he was leaving, he got to know Peter Flanigan quite well. He was a former school teacher from County Cavan. Flanigan, too, had been deposed of his original way of life and was forced into tramping to Dublin in search of work. He had read and digested every bit of Wolfe Tone's *Autobiography* and was particularly fond of a budding young poet by the name of William Allingham whom he had taught at Killeshandra in County Cavan. When Flanigan first met Brian he knew somehow that despite a lack of learning this young lad would go places and had some spunk. As they lifted ties, pounded spikes, and shoveled gravel, they talked and talked of the famine, old ways, death, women, Wolfe Tone, poetry, nature and of America—most of all of America.

"Look me lad, this young chap Allingham, the poet, I was telling you about, he's beginning to make a name for himself you know. Well, his father owns several timber ships that sail to Canada. I heard he was taking emigrants over to prevent going across the sea empty."

"How much does he want?"

"Ay, no more than three pound."

"I got nearly that saved now."

"Well, I'll tell you, me lad, Canada beats Soyer's Soup Kitchen."

"Ah, don't even talk to me of the soup kitchens of Dublin!"

It took Brian several weeks to get up his nerve to tell his sister of his intentions. When he told Teresa one windy evening in March that he was going on Allingham's ship to Canada, his sister looked like she had been sentenced to death. Her little face was all wrinkled the way it was when Dad died.

"Don't take it that way now. When I get situated in America, I'll send passage money to you. Do you hear me?"

"Aye, but why haven't you come to see me this past few months?"

"Because I had to get me head straightened out, and thanks to Peter Flanigan . . . "

"Who's he, now?"

"The older chap that I'm goin' to Canada with."

Teresa looked like a little woman now with long flowing brown hair, deep blue eyes, and a mature expression of her face probably from all the suffering she'd been through. But she took Brian's news stoically because she knew he would keep his promise of sending for her. She knew somehow they would be together again, and Elish did seem to love her like a wee sister.

"For Lord's sake, Brian, take care . . . "

"Aye, we sis, don't ya worry one bit now."

Brian left with a heavy heart and painful knot in his throat.

CHAPTER V

Bound West for Quebec

Part I

"Peter, let me tell you of a strange dream I had last night while we was waitin' for our ship."

"Aye, by all means. Please do."

"Well, I dreamed I talked with God."

"With God? How could you talk with God?"

"Well, I approached this large pole, you see. It was a pole a hundred feet high and filled with talking heads."

"Talking heads, you say?"

"Aye. One head was me father's, another Wolfe Tone's, and another me sister Teresa's and lots of others. That's the strange thing—the pole had heads of dead people and of the living."

"What were the heads saying, Brian?"

"Well, that's another strange thing, you see. I talked to all of them at the same time and even though all were speaking about different matters; I could understand all of them at once! They spoke as one voice, and that's how I know it was God."

"What were they saying?"

"All I know was each was speaking of very serious matters concerning Ireland and Irish people but all fused into something grander that wasn't Irish, but what it was I'm not sure. I think I woke up then."

"A shocking strange dream, my lad. Aye, a strange one indeed."

The pungent scent of brine, crabs and salt spray permeated the air. Something primeval oozed out of its nineteenth-century shell here on the southern coast of Ireland. Time didn't matter here. Waves pounded the sandy coves and smashed against the rocks with fury. Mist hovered over the cliff tops fringed with heather, and a Medieval wind roared and moaned through the grasses and pines. It was much wilder than Black Rock of years before with his mother and father. Just two weeks earlier a ship load of emigrants sank within sight of their relatives standing on the docks watching them go to America. Maybe these poor souls were spared a hellish two months that Peter and Brian were about to experience on the high seas of the North Atlantic. They boarded their ship with no small trepidation.

Seeing Ireland slowly disappear behind the stern of an old timber ship produced the most poignant emotions Brian's soul knew. He had left his sister behind in Dublin and his father's and mother's shallow graves in far Cavan. Gary, poor Gary was probably dead. Those long and jagged peninsulas sunk into the planet's mist, and Ireland was no more except in the dark interior of the mind.

"Ah, Brian, now don't take it so bad, man."

"Well Peter, ya know, I've left half of me in Ireland. I'm not a whole man, just half one."

"Ah, just wait till we get to Canada. Things will brighten up, you know. God, it's a choppy sea we have. It's a good job we don't have much food in our gullets."

"Aye, but me thoughts are more nauseating than any food would be."

"Ah whist now. I want ya to listen to this poem William Allingham sent to me in Dublin before we left. It's unpublished, but I know it will be in a book someday:

        "Up an airy mountain,
          Down the rushy glen,
        We daren't go-a hunting
          For fear of little men;

36

Wee folk, good folk,
   Trooping all together;
Green jacket, red cap
   And white owl's feather!

Down along the rocky shore
   Some make their home,
They live on crispy pancakes
   Of yellow tide-foam;
Some in the reeds
   Of the black mountain lake,
With frogs for their watch-dogs
   All night awake."

"Ah Peter, what kind of Ireland is Allingham writing about? For Lord's sake, it isn't the Ireland I remember with death and suffering and rot!"

"Don't you see, Brian, that it *is* an Ireland we all know that he is writing about? Amidst all that sorrow back there we still have our dreams, and we still know an Ireland in the back of our minds that *could be* heaven on earth. That's the Ireland Allingham is writing about. Some call it utopia. Wolfe Tone did. I suppose you haven't read Walton's *Complete Angler*."

"Sure I don't read at all."

"Well, *The Complete Angler*, now, paints a picture of England that is indeed utopian. Do you know when it was written? At the height of the Cromwellian Revolution back in the seventeenth century."

"Cromwellian who?"

"Oliver Cromwell. He's the bloke that planted Presbyterians on Irish soil."

"You mean you and me?"

"Well, our descendants. It's a challenge ya know. We, as Protestants, must come to the full realization that we are Irish first, and Irish last. I imagine it's a bit like Americans on a wild continent of Indians having to become Americans at last. Lord knows the British didn't help us any during the famine."

"What about *The Complete Angler*? It's about fishin' is it?"

"Aye, fishing on peaceful streams with smoke curling from thatched cottages."

"Whist will ya. Yer talkin' about me own house!"

"Well, what I mean to say . . . There you have it! You said I was talking about your own house! That's the Ireland William Allingham is writing about in his poem. Let me finish reading it will you?"

> "High on the hill-top
> The old King sits;
> He is now so old and gray
> He's nigh lost his wits.
> With a bridge of white mist
> Columbkill he crosses,
> On his stately journeys
> From Slieveleague to Rosses;
> Or going up with music
> On cold starry nights,
> To sup with the Queen
> Of the gay Northern Lights."

"Peter, the sea's getting a mite rough, we'd better go below. Look at them rolling grey clouds will ya."

"Aye, I'll finish the poem a bit later."

They descended into the ship's dingy haul housing one hundred and twenty-two emigrants, most of whom were seasick, fever-ridden and famished. They approached the soup kettle and were given a cup of steaming but thin barley soup (already known as barely soup) and a slice of stale wheaten bread.

"Brian, I'm going to have to teach you how to read before this journey is over."

"Aye, try it if you can."

"Oh don't worry, I will."

"How will ya do it?"

"The best way is to have you memorize some lines of poetry, and then I'll show you the lines and see if you can put two and two together. You aren't dumb lad, you know. You may even write poetry someday yourself."

The grey old canvas sails topside rattled in the wind as the ship pitched from side to side. It sounded like rain was pouring down hard on the deck, and every piece of timber seemed to creak and groan like a dying whale. But the groaning of all those Irish folk was worse than the ship's. Most were seasick and some had fever and rashes like the Harris' child. They were like caged beasts taken away from a volcanic island. Days and weeks fused; sunrises and sunsets and rain and fog and calm sea and choppy sea were all part of a movable pestilence. But slowly Brian McBride, with the help of Peter Flanigan, mastered the art of reading the English language. Was Peter one of the talking heads of that hundred foot pole? What is life? What is death?

Part II

Adrift in the Mid-Atlantic

The crew of the timber ship *Pinzance* had never seen such calm. One April day flooded into another with fog, flat seas and pale suns. The ship's rigging hung laden with dripping mist. They floated somewhere over lost Atlantis of fabled fame. Spirits from fathoms below seemed to bubble up from a lost civilization, or so it seemed as one emigrant after another agonized over something lost in the misty past. Ireland, the land of their sorrow, the land of their flesh, the land of their song, the land of their faith, the land of their magic was as lost to them as any fabled Atlantis. Several older men started singing the melancholic strain of "Minstrel Boy," and it spread throughout the hull like African chants on earlier slave ships. Everyone old enough to sing, sang:

> "The minstrel boy to the war is gone
> In the ranks of death you will find him."

The mist dripping from the rigging was no match for the tears streaming from two hundred eyes in the dark hull below. Despite agonizing coughs, fevers, rashes, and sore bones, these peoples' souls bubbled up through fathoms of sorrow into a joy that no god would dare challenge. The Ireland of their mind laced with mist, green fields, curling peat smoke, and communal sharing welled up from hidden depths.

41

"Danny?" one young man asked of another. "Do ya remember back in Tyrone the wee McCarthy garson*? Nearly everyone thought him the grandson of an ancient elf. What strange green eyes the lad had."

"Aye," replied Danny. "That he did. Especially during foggy spells."

"Brian, will you listen to all this," Peter said. "It's like bloody magic. It's just like pure Allingham."

"Ah Peter, it gets me to thinking about Cavan again. God, those grand rambles I took with Teresa on Sunday afternoons after church. We'd go blackberrying on the far hedgerows and make a feast of vetch, haws and blackberries. I remember one high misty brey with Lough Gowna in the distance. We'd sit up there and stare into green space and pick wee shamrocks. Far down on one of the vales we could make out me mother hanging dripping wet pieces of wash on the hedges for to dry. We'd amble back lookin' forward to all the visitin' that was to go on that evenin' with the Harrises and the Fields, Johnny and his wife. Hot cups of tea were passed around along with steamin' spuds drippin' with creamy butter. The Fields were lucky; they left for America before the famine. That bloody auld famine! The famine it was that brought out the ugliness of the British."

"Brian, you have a point there. Friends should never let you down when you're in the mud on your knees."

Another round of "Minstrel Boy" was sung and somebody tapped with two spoons to accompany the singing:

> "His father's sword he has carried on
> And his wild heart flung behind him."

But it was all interrupted by a mother's scream, and the singing stopped. Her baby had died of the fever. It was the first day of May on the high seas of the North Atlantic. His name was Kevin Ryan, the first fatality of the voyage. They wrapped him in swaddling clothes and carried him to the main deck. Dripping mist had changed to ice, and all the ship's shrouds looked like frozen grey lead. In the bitter and sharp cold, wee Kevin Ryan was dropped into icy seas

---

* boy

42

somewhere south of Iceland and west of Ireland. How much can one mother take? How much can one nation take? We all hoped Kevin would find a happier home in fabled lands.

Back in the hull of the ship Cathy and Davis Ryan sat tear streaked and glum. Canada? For what? They may as well have died in County Wexford witnessing death darken their vision of rain and sun soaked breys. A general moaning prevailed throughout the hull. Others were sick and dying. The stench of vomit, excrement and urine was stiffling. Some hoped for the ship to sink. The irony of being Irish on a British ship bound for British Canada was too much for them.

"Will ya taste this water, Brian!"

"Oh God, it tastes of turpentine, Peter. Don't tell me the ship's company put our drinking water in turpentine drums!"

"Ah sure, the first drums were fresh and new, but they must have put reserve supplies in older drums. They didn't expect such a slow voyage."

"Ya know, Peter, we're down to auld Indian cornmeal again!"

"Ah, at least good Robert Emmet suffered a quick death at the hand of the British on the gallows of Dublin!"

"Who was he, Peter?"

"Ah sure you've heard of the likes of Emmet, Irish rebel! He was a Protestant lad who led the insurrection against the British in favor of home rule. But they captured him and hanged him in Dublin town back in 1803. Before he died he gave a brilliant speech on liberty. Then they cracked his neck."

"Why must the British oppose our independence? Why can't the Emmets and Tones ever win?"

"Because we're on the wrong island! Have you ever looked at a map of England and Ireland? Ireland looks like a scared little puppy dog about to be pinched by the claws of Wales and crunched by the head of Scotland. I sometimes think Ulster is really the puppy dog's ulser. Maybe its antrims are

43

ulserous from the crunching head of Scotland. If Ireland had been the island closest to Europe, we would have had the solid backing of the French and Germans."

"Aye, I think I see. But you don't suppose that English geographic shapes makes the English people a monster chasing after an Irish puppy dog?"

"Land shapes the mind more than you might think. But, aye, there are many other reasons, me lad. Take for instance economic . . . "

"What's wrong Peter? You look a good bit white!"

"I'm after feeling a terrible chill."

Brian felt a chill in the depths of his soul.

"I'll get you a blanket and recite some more poetry for you."

"Ah no, I don't feel in any mood for poetry, Brian."

Brian accompanied him to his bed and noticed sweat break out on Peter's forehead.

Peter grew weaker and weaker as Canadian shores slowly inched closer and the days crept by. During the month of May seven more people died, each being buried in a cold, grey sea. A hundred faces solemnly munched on Indian cornmeal by kerosene lights and sipped water flavored with turpentine as the ship rocked and pitched through endless cold ocean waters. People were beginning to think the ship was going in circles.

"Brian, if I make it to Canada, I want a decent burial in the earth."

"Ah whist will ya. You'll make it to Canada as much as I will."

"But I have rashes all over me body and swelling at the joints. I'm . . . I know I'm . . . done for."

"You'll make it to Canada. I know ya will."

Then one morning in late May somebody topside shouted *land ho!* Dozens of emigrants clammered up ladders to the frozen deck and looked to the West. The faintest trace of a thread of dark land could be seen between the waves. It was the eastern shore of Newfoundland. Dozens of fishing schooners plied through the cold green waters. All looked so bleak to eyes used to emerald green shores and misty breys. Their thought must have been the same as Cabot's or Weymouth's: America at last but how different, how stark. There were even snow drifts on the mountain tops.

"Hear this, passengers! We'll put in at Saint John's for fresh water and good food before going on to Quebec," the captain shouted.

"There's a good Englishman for ya!" Davis Ryan exclaimed.

Never before was there such singing and merriment during this voyage. Elfish eyes gleamed from blotched faces. Legs danced under salty old rags. Hands clapped with boils and leprous marks. Ireland was in their eyes again—an Ireland of all their expectations.

CHAPTER VI

Canadian Shores

As Peter Flanigan knew and explained to Brian, he was in the remission stages of Typhus fever. Maybe he had a week, perhaps two, before the disease would return to kill him. But two weeks of life along strange Canadian shores gave him reason enough to be philosophical. The ship had docked for a half day at Saint John's, enough time for cleaning down the hull and for loading fresh water, tea, salted herring, flour, and pork. The passengers stared blankly at the rocky, barren, and treeless shorelines studded with a few wooden frame buildings and some stark homes. A white church steeple rose from a distant hilltop, while gulls and gannets swooped through the grey skies. The smell of seaweed and brine permeated the crisp air. After some arguing with the captain, one extra passenger boarded. His name was Iguk, an English-speaking Eskimo from Cape Dorset who was going to Ottawa to make an official complaint. Everyone stared at this strange copper-faced man dressed in sealskins.

From the far, icy shores of Cape Dorset, Iguk had come. His fellow Eskimos thought he was wasting his efforts to complain about too many white men in the Arctic. It was to white men he must complain in the first place! He wasn't against the color of their skin so much as the color of their attitudes. Why couldn't the Eskimo stay an Eskimo? Why change his ways of hunting and his ways of praying? His people told him to stay in Cape Dorset and not go to Ottawa. Why couldn't he stay and eat his seal blubber and listen to the shamin tell of his flights to the moon and back. Why couldn't he just stay and look at the golden moon glowing over Arctic ice floes? But no, he must go. He must start to make the British aware of the fact that there are other good ways of living besides British. Baffinland is too dear to us to see it transformed into something that is no longer a wild Arctic Baffinland beset with ice floes. Iguk began to chat and mix freely with the Irishmen as the *Pinzance* plied through coastal waters off bleak eastern Newfoundland and west toward snowy Port aux Basques. All emigrants rejoiced over fresh food. Some guzzled as much as twenty cups of steaming tea and ate plateful after plateful of salted herring. Even Peter was able to enjoy a mouthful of herring and taste of fresh baked hot bread. For many, this was the first taste of life in twelve months.

"Brian, see if you could get that Eskimo chap to come over to me bunk for a chat."

"Iguk, ya mean? Ah sure he's busy laughin' and jokin' with a brave crowd of folks from Tipperary. He seems to like tea as much as we do."

"He's a handsome dark lad, indeed. I've never seen such shiny white teeth! But do try and get him over here for a wee chat."

"I'll see if I can."

Iguk fascinated the emigrants with his talk of seal, walrus and musk ox, though they knew not what these animals were. He told them story after story of being afloat on ice pans not knowing if he would ever get home alive. Somehow they understood what he meant when he told them "Aja— it was good. Aja—it was joyful."

"Sure if yer lost in yer own homeland, which is ice in yer case, it must be joyful, as ya put it," Danny Riordan said. "I remember bein' lost in the Bog of Allen. But ya know, it wasn't all that bad for a bog is still Ireland isn't it?"

"Aja, you right. Lost in homeland isn't lost," Iguk remarked.

Brian succeeded in tearing away Iguk from the laughing Tipperary crowd and brought him over to Peter.

"Ah, a shocking foine lad you are, Iguk," Peter exclaimed.

"Aja, shocking find dad you."

"Tell me now, what brings you aboard an emigrant ship?"

48

"Aja, too many white men come into Arctic with guns. Spoil our hunting. Too many white men give guns to us to have *us* spoil our hunting. They want us to sell hides so white lady wear fur in warm South. Too many white men tell us how to pray."

"Aye, but what can you do?"

"Eyes, I tellum in Ottawa to keep white men out."

"Ottawa may not listen if there's a crown involved."

"Ottawa listen or I break crown involved."

Peter roared with laughter for the first time since he left Cavan. He laughed so hard his decaying teeth ached. This Eskimo chap had spunk. Maybe the Irish and Eskimos together would make England listen. Both peoples had English ways forced upon them.

"Tell me Iguk," questioned Brian, "how did ya get to St. John's, or is that yer home?"

"Aja, no. Cape Dorset, Baffinland. I come down on other ship to St. John's."

"Oh aye, aye."

"Eyes, eyes," said Iguk pointing to his eyes. "You people like eyes? We do too. Best part of seal. I go to Ottawa on seal furs I sell."

"Eyes you say . . . oh, aye," Peter chuckled.

"Eyes," Iguk grunted.

The ship entered the mouth of the painfully gleaming Saint Lawrence River after two day's sail from St. John's. They inched past Anticosti Isle, ice covered and barren. The Irish had never experienced such cold weather in May, but, after braving the harshest winter on record in Ireland, they were somewhat used to it.

"Irishmen! Come! Come topside," Iguk shouted, holding a pipe in his hand. "Look, seals! Seals I tell you about."

"Will ya look at the white one," Davis Ryan remarked. "It looks like a banshee itself."

"When we hunt seal in North," Iguk explained, "we share all its parts, even the heart. If we share the heart, we call ourselves heart partners. But we never kill more seal than we can eat, and that is why white mens' guns are bad. His whiskey bad too—we can't hold it—it makes us go mad."

"Aye," I said, "I've known some Irish to go mad with it too."

Twenty or so Irish men and boys calmly stared at the strange whiskered harbor seals splashing about the rocks of Anticosti. They could see the surf crashing against the shore and longed to step out onto the land—solid land. If only they could have left those creaking timbers back at St. John's.

That evening they experienced a brilliant, fiery Canadian sunset casting aglow the entire icy waters of the upper Saint Lawrence. Stars peppered the evening sky and a rising full moon gleamed with its pock marks looking like some strange new invading planet. Iguk smoked his walrus tusk pipe with aromatic native tobaccos while Brian supported Peter ever so slowly pacing the deck.

"Iguk," Brian inquired, "would ya let me have a puff of yer pipe?"

"Eyes. Here!"

Brian puffed on the pipe and blew out a highly aromatic smoke. Peter hadn't smelled pipe tobacco in over twelve months. Not thinking of his disease, Peter asked to have a wee puff to which Iguk readily consented.

"Oh aye, oh God aye," Peter chuckled out in raucous fashion. He coughed a little and took another long puff on the walrus pipe and handed it back to the Eskimo and beamed with self-contentment.

"You smoke pipe like true Eskimo native," Iguk remarked.

"We Irish are pipe smokers, but after a good bit of hardship during the past year or so we haven't been able to afford tobacco for our pipes."

"Me no buy tobacco—make from ground plants. When we go ashore I show you some."

"Oh aye, aye."

"Eyes, eyes. Wish I had seal eyes to eat."

Iguk looked over the bow of the ship and wished he had brought along his harpoon. Surely he could have killed a seal at Anticosti. Think of the feast they would have had. He could have made the Irishmen his heart partners.

"Iguk," Brian questioned, "do ya miss yer home at Cape Dorset?"

"What kind of question that? If I not at home, as you can see, I miss my home!"

"Ah sure. Peter and I miss County Cavan. God, I remember goin' to church listening to Reverend Samuel as though it were yesterday. He'd remind us of our weak human natures and never to look at women until ya married one of them."

"What kind of preaching that? If you see woman, you see her. Maybe even you have her. What wrong with that?"

"Iguk, we have our morals, you have yers." Brian stated cooly if not sanctimoniously.

"Why so many people live together in one ship? You share women then, don't you?"

"Ah no, sex is the last thing ya think of when there's disease, sufferin', and death."

"But just today I see Irish woman suckling child with her big breasts. You no look?"

Brian had looked, many times during the voyage. How could he not? He sometimes had life-like dreams especially if that dark haired girl from Cavan got on his brains. His thoughts wandered back to what Reverend Samuel had said and what the Eskimo was saying. What could he do but close it all out of his mind? Morals is a confusing subject especially when the whole world is so upside down.

"Iguk, do yous have any sports in Cape Dorset?"

"Sometimes we kick stuffed seal gut over ice."

"Oh aye. God, just about every Sunday afternoon we boys from the country would play football with Bellturbet or Ballybay. God, I remember one match. It was a drivin' rain. It was rainin' so hard ya could hardly see the muddy field. We was kickin' the ball about until its leather almost burst when what happens but a brave lot of barking blood-hounds çome runnin' out on the playin' field and English gentlemen go gallopin' over the field followin' the dogs who is chasin' hares or foxes. Well, I'll tell ya, it was a sea of mud, a sea of mud. But they didn't stop our football match, they didn't."

Peter asked Iguk for another puff on the pipe as he huddled under a blanket and sat on the deck listening with all ears. He hadn't lived so intensely since he taught at Killeshandra.

"And then after the match we'd all go home for spuds and wash up. Aye, we'd put on our best and walk out in the evening air for the country dance hall."

"Pure Allingham, me lad. Pure Allingham," Peter mused.

"Pure Alleyham, pure Alleyham," Iguk imitated.

"Aye. When we'd arrive at the dance hall, the fiddlin' and stompin' of feet filled the rafters. We'd dance around the floor until everything was a blur, a bloody blur. Them was the days. And walkin' home under the moonlight, ya really wouldn't mind havin' to work the fields on the morrow. I was just getting old enough to enjoy life when hell closed in on Ireland just like it said it would in the Bible with famine and plague."

"Would ya mind if we all went below," Peter asked. "I'm after getting a brave chill."

Iguk and Brian helped Peter down the ladder covered with brine to his bunk and gave him a hot mug of tea. He swilled it loudly.

"We have mug-up, right," Iguk asked.

"Mug-up," Peter mused, "Aye—mug-up is a good term for it. Aye a bloody good term for it—having tea. Brian, after Canada, you'll have to go to Boston, ya know."

"Are them many Irish people there?"

"Aye."

One of the crew members told the emigrants that they just passed Tadoussac where they would return for timber after they unloaded passengers at Grosse Isle near Quebec City. Several of the passengers including Brian climbed up the ladders to look at moonlit Canadian shores. They could readily see the dense black spruce forests and rocky cliffs. The high Laurentians rose in the distance like dolphins in the sea. The air was pure and invigorating. Each breath seemed to clear the lungs of all their putrefaction. When Brian returned to the hull, all of this Saint Lawrence joy dissipated like fog under a painful sun. Peter was dying, and his new friend Iguk was broken out in rashes.

"Two more heads for your pole, Brian," Peter rasped.

"Ah don't talk to me of me foolish dreams. They mean nothing, Peter."

"I, of all people, gave Iguk the bloody auld Typhus. Now he can't go to Ottawa to break their crown'"

"Me go alright, even if I die at grandmother Victoria's house."

"Iguk, get off this ship as soon as we dock and go into the forests and get well," Brian pleaded. "And as for yer givin' Iguk the disease—how do ya know it was you, Peter. Ya haven't given it to me, have ya?"

"I've taught you to read and come three thousand miles to teach Iguk to die," Peter grumbled. "May God judge me for the miserable creature that I am. What the hell kind of teacher am I, anyway?" Peter blankly stared at wooded shores as thick as the tangled strips of woods separating the green fields of Ireland.

The ship slowly edged up to Grosse Isle in a dense fog thirty miles from Quebec City where the passengers were ordered to disembark. From the shoreline, all heard the funereal beating of a drum which served as a primitive fog-horn. Two men sat on a cliff and beat a large drum regularly looking like something out of a dream. The crew had to carry five emigrants off in stretchers; Peter Flanigan was one of them. Brian lingered on the deck long after the last passenger left. He couldn't face stepping off a ship that had once docked in Ireland and was now deep into North America. He knew that the moment he stepped off the *Pinzance* onto strange soil, he was stepping out of Ireland, perhaps forever. The gnawing worry of Peter's deteriorating condition pulled him toward the shore. But, maybe he should ask the captain if he could return to Ireland and his little Teresa. He'd work as a crew member. Surely he had been a fool for coming all this way. Why not go back and work on The Cork railway line and visit his sister and Elish once a week? Elish could have taught him to read.

"You come quick," Iguk shouted from the docks.

Brian grabbed his satchel and ran down the gangplank to see what was the matter. Iguk snatched his arm and dragged him over to a smelly old shanty where dying immigrants from this voyage and others lay moaning. They found Peter on the floor in a dark corner.

"Peter! My God, why have they put you in this dingy auld place?"

"To die, me lad, to die!" Peter barely rasped out, "I want you to bring back word to Cavan if you ever return that I have seen this vast America and talked with her natives. This new land is not a scared puppy dog . . . this new land has . . . strength . . . this new land . . . " His head rolled to the side and his blank eyes stared up at Canadian cobwebs. His spirit liberated itself from a pasty shell of a body covered with boils, rashes and swellings.

"Where's a minister, a minister please," Brian shouted frantically. A French Canadian official explained, "Nous n'avons point de curés, monsieur. J'ai triste."

"What did he say, Iguk?"

"I think he say no minister. Let us go. They bury him."

"Not in an unmarked grave. Not Peter Flanigan!"

"Let us go. They bury him."

"England, just you wait."

"Least he not get buried in sea!"

"Now where do I go? Where do I go? England, just you wait!"

Iguk and Brian were led out of the shanty and told to get medical clearance for leaving Grosse Isle. Brian was half tempted to go to Cape Corset and fight the English there, but his mind was whirling through space.

"Iguk, please don't you die. Go to the woods and get better and then go to Ottawa."

"Eyes."

When the doctor examined them, he let Brian pass but not Iguk. The Eskimo was too far gone.

"If he can't leave, I won't either."

"Monsieur, c'est les règles."

"What are règles? Regulations ya mean? This man is not Irish, he is a native Canadian. Let him pass!"

When Brian threatened to punch the doctor in the mouth, he finally let Iguk pass. They were shuttled across in a small boat to the misty north shore of the Saint Lawrence. They remained silent for quite some time until Iguk blurted out, "I go woods, get better. You go Quebec, get work."

Iguk trudged into a misty spruce and tamarack forest, and Brian never saw the Eskimo again. Whether he got better and went to Ottawa remained a mystery until Brian's dying day. So here I am in Canada, Brian thought as he stood at the spot where Iguk left him. It was chilly, really chilly. The spruce trees creaked in spring breezes, and the great Saint Lawrence lapped its stoney shores. Brian looked across at Grosse Isle and saw the masts of the *Pinzance*. Each time he looked back at that ship he thought of Peter Flanigan now rotting in some fresh grave. Have I lived through all this only to stand on Canadian shores, he thought to himself. Brian slowly ambled south toward Quebec City until he came upon a carriage road on which he walked at yet a faster pace. He walked southward to where he did not know. He walked toward the great Niagara Falls which he heard tell of from crew members. Maybe, he thought, if he listened carefully he could hear the roar of thundering Niagara. There's America for you, the roar of Niagara. Iguk, there's America for you—men of seals and ice pans. This land is strong. Peter was right. Look at those huge black cliffs. Look at this big river. Why it had power enough to wash away all of Ireland. Is that what I'm doing—washing away Ireland?

As he approached a small village, Brian saw darkly clad farmers out in some distant fields covered with rich, milky haze. They seemed to be tilling. Tilling for what? If ever I am to get to the United States, here's my chance. Maybe I could work for a fortnight and then travel to Boston or New York. I think Peter said that's where all the Irish were. But why am I leaving all those Irish at Grosse Isle? My mind is in a daze, a bloody auld daze. He walked up to a wooden farm house and knocked on the door:

"Pardon, mame. Would ya be needin' any help in the fields?"

"Pardon, Monsieur, je ne parle pas Anglais."

"*Me*, I am farmer. I want to work."

"Farmah? Farmer, farmer, oh!—vous voulez dire "fermier" Vous etes fermier?"

"Fermieh, fermieh, oh! You mean fermier means "farmer!" Yes, me fermieh."

"Attendez. Je vais chercher mon mari."

Why did the silly woman leave me, Brian wondered. Peter and me father must have been insane to tell me to come to America. Why America? They don't even speak English. A tall, husky Canadian farmer approached the door. He was wearing a heavy wollen shirt, a beaver cap, and moccasins and looked like he was half Indian.

"Eh, Monsieur. Entrez entrez. Mangez avec nous!"

"I don't speak French, monsewer."

"Entrez. Venez ici. Vous etes le bienvenu!"

"Enter, do you mean?"

"Enter, yees, enter. Mangez—eeet."

"Oh aye, oh God aye."

Brian entered his first wooden frame house ever and sat down at a maplewood table surrounded with three daughters, husband and wife. Plates of buttered carrots, potatoes, and trout were passed around.

"Vous etes fermier, monsieur?"

"Farmer. Me farmer from Ireland. Brian McBride's me name."

"D'Irlande, vous avez dites. D'Irlande! Etes-vous malade? Avez-vous le Typhus??" The Frenchman gestured pointing to the face and body. Brian caught his meaning.

"No, Monsewer. I do not have typhus." Brian took off his shirt and stood up and turned around. This must have been proof positive that he was well as not a mark showed on his thin but strong white body.

"Mangez, EEET. Mangez, Bree-an. J'ai triste, mais j'ai pense que . . . puisque vous etes Irlandais . . . Nous nous appellons Simon. Brian only understood "Mangez," and mangez he did. The three daughters eyed Brian amorously. The oldest one looked something like Teresa. They were teenagers with soft brown eyes and long flowing hair.

"Monsewer, I would like to work. I'm a potato farmer. Fermier of potatoes."

"Oh, vous voulez dire que vous etes fermier de pommes de terres. Potatoes—pommes de terre."

"Aye, a farmer of pommes de terre."

"Vous voulez traviller ici aux champs? Eh bien, vous pouvez travailler ici. Nous sommes en train de planter des pommes de terres, et nous avons besoin de travailleurs. Monsieur, yooo wek hehr," Monsieur Simon entreated. After dinner Brian was given old work clothes, and he changed in a room next to the girls. They stretched out on the bed

57

with their elbows behind their backs giving full of their firm breasts under tight sweaters. Monsieur Simon, Brian's new employer, shouted, "Bree-an. Venez. Allons aux champs!"

Brian's work of planting potato seeds in Canadian fields was marvelled at. He was quick and seemed to work without effort. "Forte bien!" his fellow workers would say. As he worked, he stared out at the misty blue Laurentians and listened to the plaintive notes of song sparrows. Delicate blue flowers fringed the rolling fields; it was almost like being back in Cavan. The air was so rich and heavy and sweet it was like chocolate. But by the time he returned each evening to the Simon's household, he was exhausted or epuisé as he learned to say. At nine o'clock he was ready for bed and passed out in moments. One evening Dorine Simon, the eldest daughter, drapped a sheet around her naked body and gently knocked on Brian's door. He thought he heard the knocking in his sleep, but he wasn't sure and of course made no response. She knocked again but no response came from within. She took it as an insult and huffed back to her room. As she lay crying in her pillow with tears running down her olive-skin face, she knew she would never speak to or even look at Brian. He thinks his white, white body is too good for me, she thought. Well, I know different. Irishmen are no better than Frenchmen she felt. He must be crazy.

After the chilly planting season was over Brian was given five British pounds for his hard work. He planted more seed than any Canadian and worked harder than most in firming up the brown soil over the potato drills. He had loved his work as it made him forget all that he had been through. There's nothing like dirt on the fingers to forget agonies of the past.

"Au revoir, Monsewer Simon. C'était un plaisir de travailler ici." Brian stumbled out with a thick Irish accent. But at least he picked up enough French to get by with. After a twenty mile walk, he entered the gates of Quebec City walking its narrow and winding lanes surrounded by quaint Norman buildings. British soldiers stamped down the streets and Brian shook his fist and hooted at them. One shouted back, "What's yer name, bloke?"

"Brian McBride, ya scoundrel!"

"Go back to Ireland, ya scum ye."

He entered a little cafe and ordered a bowl of chick pea soup and asked if there was any way of getting to Boston from Quebec.

"Mais oui, bien entendu. Il faut aller à Montréal et puis par "stage coach" à Albany et c'est bien facile d'aller à Boston d' Albany."

"Oh aye, je pense que je . . . comprend . . . aye."

He left blue skied Canada in early June, 1847. He only hoped that Iguk was still somehow alive and regaining his strength in the woods.

CHAPTER VII

North Square Slums and Walden Woods

"Excuse me sir, where might I find lodgin'," Brian asked a gruff sort of person with buck teeth and puffy cheeks.

"Irish scum usually live in North Square," was all he answered while pointing in the general direction of the forboding ghetto.

Brian wearily trudged along the strange streets of the city of Boston feeling downcast and tired after a long journey from Montreal. He wondered what kind of work he would find here and how long it would be before he could send for Teresa. Boston, America—so this is America with all its galloping carriages, fur collared gentlemen, red brick buildings, coal smoke, and old glory. By late afternoon his knees were wobbly from walking over stone streets and brick sidewalks. Then it was that he saw some dingy red brick buildings laced with wooden balconies, hanging wash, and dirty alleyways. It wasn't long before he heard the familar Irish brogue and saw red raced drunkards stumbling along the shabby sidewalks.

The two IRA rebels scrounged through their sacks to find some crusts of bread and a thin flask of brandy. The middle of their second day in hiding was foggy with a glaring sun. They could hardly see the rising breys leading up to Slieve Gullion.

"Ah Michael, let's have a spot of lunch a wee while, now. That poor bastard made it to Boston anyway."

"Aye Steven, that he did, but I'll tell you why he went West and ... What's that? ... Will ya listen to them firin' away at Fork Hill. We're gona have to join our lads on the morrow, ya know. But we might get plugged today what with this thick fog."

"Aye, there's not much we could do in a fog—we'd likely tramp into the hands of the British without knowin' it. Ya know, I wouldn't mind fightin' along with a bloke like Brian McBride."

"Ah sure, Steve, McBride was a Protestant and we're to drive every Protestant pig into the Irish sea, are we not?"

"Aye, but if all the Protestants were like this here Brian ... but, anyway, what happened to him in Boston?"

He asked an old washerwoman with curly white whiskers on her chin where he might rent a room, and she pointed with her broom to an old and dingy office with the decrepit remains of a County Mayo spinning wheel. Kevin O'Reilly, a grey haired and strong chinned proprietor of the building, asked for five dollars in advance for a room overlooking clotheslines strung above a back alley.

"Five dollars. I have only a pound note." He had spent the rest of his Canadian earnings in getting to Boston by way of Albany where he had lodged for a day along the shores of the Hudson River.

"Aye, one pound note will do. Ya got a bed, wash bowl and towel. The one pound will pay for thirty days and no more. I suppose you'll be lookin' for work. A lot of Irish works with the railway."

"Aye, I'll go and have a look. That's what I done in Dublin."

"Yer from Dublin are ye?"

"Ah no, County Cavan."

"Oh aye. And ya worked in Dublin afterwards."

"Aye. Me sister's still there."

"Well, ya got some excuse to go back should ya not like it here. We got lots of sick people here too, ya know. They brought the typhus with them, a brave lot of folks did."

"Aye. I suppose they would. A good many died on our ship."

"Did ya land here in Boston?"

"No, Canada."

"I see. That's illegal ya know."

"Don't talk to me of what's illegal! The whole world is illegal."

He trudged up the steps looking for room 46 and passed rooms full of people sitting idly and coughing and wheezing. Some were drinking homebrew and singing the tired remains of some country ballad. His room was tiny, and he couldn't understand why there were so many bunks in so small a room. Cobwebs hung from the cracked plaster ceiling, and one wee window overlooked a back alley of wooden balconies and clotheslines. From the window, he could hear coughing, moaning and some melancholic fiddle music. Some people walked the alleys with vinegar soaked handkerchiefs over their faces in an apparent attempt to ward off malignant fever. Muddy puddles in the alley dimly reflected sooty brick chimneys while dirty pigeons fluttered above the grey shingled roofs. He overheard some people talking about the midget Prime Minister Lord John Russell and how their relative's death had to be attributed to him. The voices talked of President Polk and how he wasn't much better. What did America want with all that land in Mexico anyway? Didn't they have enough? America was just another England as far as that goes—the Great American Empire where English only must be spoken—where Mexican territory was enticing but not the people—where Indians had to be shot to make room for democracy! Brian had never heard such bitterness before, but then he, like all others there in North Square, had lost so much dear to him.

Brian threw his satchel of clothing and a handwritten poem by Allingham on his bunk bed and trudged down the steps to ask the landlord some questions about the railroads.

"Where did ya say that railroad was now?"

"The Boston and Fitchburg Terminal—that-a-way, lad," the landlord said. "Hey, did you say you was from Cavan?"

"Aye, indeed I did."

"Well, some folks stayed here a while back and took up farming near Concord. I s'pose ya wouldn't know them though—the Fields, Johnny and the missis."

"Oh aye, aye indeed. Johnny Field. Sure he was me neighbor. Was he a tall man with dark hair and brown eyes?"

"Aye, that he was, lad. He looks a good bit like you."

"Where's Concord?"

"Sure, not far from here, 'bout twenty miles to the west."

"Ya brightened me day, man."

Brian left the apartment house and trekked down to the Boston and Fitchburg Railway Terminal and asked for work telling of his employment back in Dublin. He was hired right off and looked forward to starting work early the next morning.

He climbed the creaking steps of his apartment building and walked down a dark hallway to his room. Passing one door left ajar, he couldn't help but see a middle-aged man and woman making love on a dirty old carpeted floor. Their groaning could be heard as far as his room. When he opened his door, he was surprised to see seven people in his room: three women, two men, and two children.

"What are ya doin' here," he asked them.

"This here's our room, and you was added to it," a child said coldly.

"But we can't all fit in here!"

"Indeed we can. You should see the room one flight up. It has nine people in it, and it's smaller than this," said an older woman with a hairy mole on her face. One of the men was stone drunk with a bottle of poteen at his side. The three women were slovenly and smelled like rotting corpses. The other man was asleep on one of the bunks, and the two children played idly on the floor with a black old cockroach that ambled slowly toward the bottle of poteen. One of the boys looked like he had typhus rashes. Brian thought to himself that he would sleep in these shambles and spend the bulk of the day elsewhere. If only he could find Johnny Field.

He didn't sleep much that night as everybody but the children snored loudly. It wasn't yet sunrise and all he could do was lie there and think. At least when he was at sea, the sound of the creaking timbers and splashing waves offset the snoring. And he was spoiled by his Canadian room all to himself. Perhaps he should have stayed in Quebec. Those Simon daughters were lovely, and he had every intention of striking up a conversation with . . . what was her name . . . Dorine, but he was always so tired after planting seed in the fields. He had worked hard. But for what? To come to these wretched slums? Peter Flanigan, you were bloody well crazy to have me come to Boston. We're hated here, and we hate each other. We're too crowded together with nothing to do but get drunk and tend to our lusts and dream about green Ireland with its open fields and breys and mist on the lakes.

God, I remember when we was smaller, Teresa and I, just rambled down the country lanes in the pale sunlight peeking through grey clouds. The hedgerows glowed with cranberry-red leaves and sweet smellin' peat smoke filled the air. I hadn't ever seen it snow in Ireland until that cursed potato famine came and rotted our souls. Here we all lie in Boston. For God's sake, why Boston? What good am I doing in Boston when I should be back in Ireland?

Rain started to patter the roof at daybreak and water dripped through the leaking rafters onto the bunks. Rain streaked past the window like grey bars. Brian got up and dressed long before anybody awakened. He paced along the wet sidewalks in the misty rain toward the Boston and Fitchburg Railway Terminal. He was told by his foreman that he would be working a stretch of track near Concord by a pond and that he would have to sleep in some shanties built nearby.

"Ya mean I don't have to stay in them dingy auld slums at North Square?"

"Aye, ya'd better run back and get yer belongings and check out. Be back here in thorty minutes."

Brian ran all the way with his heart and lungs bursting. He tasted blood in his mouth he ran so hard. When he asked where his satchel was in his room, the woman with the hairy mole told him to get the feck out. When he asked the land-lord for his money back he was told to go to hell. He ran back to the station and was told he was late and unless he could catch up to departing work cars, he was out of a job. He ran down along the glistening railroad tracks at full speed and grabbed the cold iron railing of the caboose and almost lost his grip. For a split second he was staring into grinding steel wheels, but he managed to struggle onto the moving platform of the caboose and fell down on the floor panting for life. He hobbled forward to the work cars and sat down next to a grey haired and toothless chap:

"Me name's Brian McBride from County Cavan," he said panting deeply and extending his hand.

"Sam Brady here. I'm from Drogheda."

"Oh aye, I think we walked through there on the way to Dublin last December."

"I came here last December and have been workin' on this Fitchburg line since January. How is it back home?"

"Sure everybody is still in a state of terror. Bodies are buried in fresh graves all over the countryside."

"I've heard tell the famine is over."

"Sure it wasn't when we left."

66

"Oh aye, but it's June now, lad. Time has sped."

"Aye, that's true. I hope me sister Teresa is keeping well. I'll soon send for her."

"What age has she?"

"Seven."

"Better to let her stay, lad. Let her stay till she's a good bit older. The voyage across the grey auld Atlantic would kill her."

"Ah no, she and I are too close."

"*Were* close, lad, *were*. It's June now and time has sped."

"Time don't change them kind of things."

Sam pulled out his pipe and lit up and thought carefully over his gummed-out words:

"Lad, just wait a wee while anyway."

"Oh aye, I haven't got no money. A landlord kept it on me."

"Well, there ya are."

After what seemed like hours of rattling along the bumpy tracks and smelling whiffs of coal smoke, the train stopped along the shores of a small lake called Walden Pond. Large white pines shimmered in the misty haze. The waters looked blue at a distance and yellow-green nearby. Someone was out in a boat playing a flute.

"Brian, ya know, when we was in Drogheda, we used to go to the Mountains of Mourne once a year to lakes like this one. I remember one misty lake with Slieve Gullion rising up in the distance. We used to ramble about looking at the ferns, heather, and pines. We'd only go once a year, but that one day on the mountain meant so much to us."

Michael and Steven stopped talking about the diary for awhile to watch the sun set over the cleared valleys below while Slieve Gullion reddened in silence. They ate some rations and walked out to take a drink from the nearby stream. Michael thought he saw a farmer watching them from a lower vale but wasn't sure. For some reason he didn't bother telling Steven.

"Why did ya go once a year to the Mountains of Mourne, Sam?"

"Ah, just to get away from it and think for a change, that's all."

"Aye, Teresa and I used to do that by climbing up the breys and picking blackberries. We'd come home to a house full of people talkin' of crops and tellin' stories. Johnny Field was always likely to be there and the Harrises."

"Johnny Field did ya say? John Field from Cavan?"

"Aye, oh aye, that's right. I heard tell he was in these parts."

"Indeed he is. After we finish work tonight, we'll go over to his bog for a visit."

"Aye, t'will be somethin' to look forward to."

They got out of the work cars and approached a pile of ties or sleepers and rails. They were to repair a bad patch of road bed above Walden Pond. Sam, Brian, and ten others loosened the rails, lifted them off, dug up sleepers, shoveled gravels in hollows, laid down new sleepers, and drove in the rails with big iron spikes. Brian was all sweaty and greasy by six o'clock, quitting time. The sun was low in a yellow sky as they approached a shanty in the woods. Nearby Brian and Sam washed off in a brook and changed out of their railroad overalls.

"We'll do a wee callying* at the Fields tonight, eh what lad?"

"Ah, sure Johnny will be a great sight for me eyes after so long."

"Do ya pipe smoke? I got a spare pipe and tobacco if ya like."

"Oh aye, the last time I smoked was on a walrus tusk pipe of a poor old Eskimo. Lord knows what ever happened

---

* visiting

68

to him."

"In Ireland, lad?"

"Comin' across the Saint Lawrence," Brian explained as he puffed on American tobacco. "This is delightful stuff, aye."

"We don't have no Eskimos here, but I have seen an occasional Penobscot Indian selling his wares."

"That so?"

The two men tramped across the fields and spongy meadows into a dense wood filled with ferns and mosses. Sam pointed out that the woods consisted of a pleasing mixture of pines, maples, birches, and oaks which I thought ᵊrather strange that he should know. He had grown to know and love his new land. At about sunset they arrived at a wee cabin and saw Johnny sitting in front of it smoking a pipe and staring into a nearby bog.

"Well, if it isn't Johnny Field himself," Brian shouted.

"Brian, Brian McBride? What brings ya here? Kathleen, Kevin, come, it's Eddie McBride's son with old Sam Brady from Drogheda." Brian put his arms around Johnny and Kathleen. "I see ya got a new babe, Johnny!"

"Aye," John Field replied. "Born here in America. They call me John over here, Brian. It's more dignified, ya see."

Brian was hurt to the quick, but he didn't let on that he was.

"Oh, I see."

"It's just the way it is over here."

Brian told him of his father's and mother's grim death and of the voyage across the sea and that Teresa was still in Dublin with her cousin. He didn't even mention Gary figuring that "John" would not have remembered anyway.

"And how is it with you over here, John?"

"Grand, grand. I'm gettin' ten dollars a week fer boggin'. We're eatin' here better than we did over in miserable old Cavan." Brian was hurt all the more. "Tea, coffee, milk, butter and even beef!"

"Well, I'll tell ya. I was eatin' spuds and trout and bacon up in Canada."

John didn't seem to listen to him for he didn't ask any questions about Canada. Sam Brady puffed on his pipe and sensed the friction.

"Things is even worse in I'reland I hear, Brian."

"Aye, but let's not talk of Ireland now. There are more Irish over here than in Ireland so it seems."

"That's why some Bostonians is callin' Boston the cesspool of the world with all its Irish slums. Ya wouldn't believe those slums Brian!" John put it.

"Sure it's the British that caused it anyway," Brian cooly remarked.

"Ah sure they didn't cause the famine now, Brian," John added.

"No, they didn't cause the famine, but they didn't relieve the sufferin' much," Brian said. "But yous is eatin' well over here, eh? Beef, tea, coffee?"

"Aye, we are. But ya know, some strange bloke by the name of Henry Thoreau who lives in a hut not far from here . . . "

"Is he the one that plays the flute out in his boat?" Sam interrupted.

"I could not say. But he told me that if I'd stop eatin' beef and drinkin' tea, my needs would be less, and I wouldn't have to work so hard at boggin'."

Brian scratched his chin and thought a moment: "It seems to me I've heard that before. Simple needs and simple wants. Isn't that what the British preached to us during the famine? I remember . . . " Brian couldn't go on but simply asked, "Why didn't you tell Mr. Henry whatever that yous didn't have no beef to eat back in Ireland?"

"Ah sure I wouldn't question back to a college educated man, Brian. Besides, I hear tell he's writin' some sort of book about livin' in the woods and declarin' personal independence."

"The book sounds interesting, but he doesn't know much about what's going on in Ireland, does he?"

"Ireland is of no importance here, Brian," John stated cooly.

"Some think it's important," Sam said in a low voice. "There's an Irish Relief Agency in Boston, ya know."

"Relief?? If them Irish folk would only get out and work, they wouldn't need no relief."

"Sit down will yous," Kathleen implored. "Have some tea, hot beef and fresh bread."

"Aye, sit down, eat," John added.

After a frustrating evening's chat with the Fields, Sam and Brian returned to their wee shanty, crawled under the blankets of their bunk beds and chatted as stars shone through the window. The fresh pine wood in the shanty was pleasing to Brian's nostrils.

Sensing Brian's melancholy, Sam Brady asked,

"Did I ever tell you of me cousin back in Dublin be the name of James Brady?"

"No ya didn't."

"Well now, he was a foine card I tell ya. He worked in an auld flour mill near the Royal Canal, but he just hated his work what with comin' home all white with flour every night. His home, now, was just next door to the mill, and he'd much prefer sittin' home takin' a sup a tay and readin' some foine poetry, though I think it was fer show, for I don't rightly remember his ever learnin' how to read."

"By foine poetry do ya means the likes of Allingham . . . a poet I read and lost . . . "

"Ah sure, how would you know, now? But, anyway, twelve hours of hard work in the flour mill was just too much for him to take everyday, sure it was. Well, it got so that he'd scheme of ways of gettin' out of work until he came across

71

a foine plan. He'd just hop over the mill wall into his back-yard in the middle of the work day and brew up some tay and light up his pipe by his peat fire. His woife asked if he hadn't better get back to the mill and he'd just say that surely they thought he was at work anyway.

One day, after he had started raisin' flowers and tomato plants in his backyard on the mill's time, some inspectors or somethin' must have noticed he wasn't at work. Didn't they come and knock on his front door askin' for him. Well did he ever light up over the mill wall in a shockin' hurry! Except he caught himself in the ivy vines and the buttons of his fork had all jarred loose. Didn't he look a foolish sight up there straddling the wall twisted in ivy with his fork wide open."

Brian giggled with laughter and asked whatever became of him.

"Well, shrewd auld James Brady, after he was laid off work, just sent his wife to work instead, and as far as I know he's still back there in Dublin raisin' tomato plants, readin' poetry and smokin' his pipe."

"James Brady sounds a little like that American bloke that was talkin' to Field what with claimin' his independence and all that."

"Well ya know, I just couldn't tell ya," Sam responded. "Brian me boy, we had better get some sleep before the morrow's hard work. But whenever we have a spare mo-ment, I'd like to teach ya the names of some of these here plants and trees. They're beautiful things, ya know."

"Aye, perhaps there may be time."

During the next several days at work, the routine of lifting ties, repairing railbeds along the Fitchburg line grew tiresome and boring. Somehow Johnny Field wasn't the happy man he knew back in Ireland. In fact, the entries in the diary (now with the IRA rebels) between August, 1847 and August, 1852 were far and few between. The only thing of interest to Michael, the reader on the slopes of Slieve Gullion, was that Sam and Brian talked about the West.

They believed Horace Greeley was right. The lure of the open praires, big skies, and snow covered mountains was like a haunting dream to Brian now surrounded by grey skies, mist, and confining woods. Even County Cavan had a greater sense of space than these damp Massachusetts woodlands. Somehow the damp Walden woods became as restricting as the slums of North Square. Slowly Sam Brady convinced Brian that Teresa was better off in Dublin and that Brian should experience America to its fullest and return to Ireland someday when Teresa approached womanhood. Brian wrote his sister through Elish at Rathmines several times but strangely enough received no reply. You would think that Elish would have written something back for Teresa, but she didn't.

"What's that noise, Steven?"

"I don't know, Michael. I'll have a look."

A white-haired farmer with a stubble of whiskers approached the cowshed carrying a brown sack.

"Who goes there?" they shouted.

"A friend, that's all, a friend."

They frisked the old farmer to see if he had any weapons and found only five bottles of Guiness.

"What brings ya here?" Michael asked.

"I knew yous was up here. I just live down the brey, and I thought I'd bring yous somethin' to drink."

"How do we know you ain't no British informer?"

"An old feeble Catholic man the likes of me," he said making the sign of the cross, *"hardly engages in dorty politics, now. Besides I help raise the tricolors at Crossmaglen when I'm down there."*

They opened the bottles of dark Guiness and drank with long, thirsty swallows. Steven started singing an old IRA rebel song:

"On the Galtimore Mountains
Not far far away
I'll tell you a story
That happened one day
About a young colleen,
Her age was sixteen,
And she sported her colors
White, orange and green.
Then a young soldier
By chance came that way.
He spied the young maiden
With colors so gay.
He rode along side her
Jumped from his machine
All determined to capture
The flag of Sinn Fein.
You'll not get these colors
Until I am dead.
I'll fight by the glenside
It's plain to be seen,
And I'll die for these colors
White, orange and green.
The bold English soldier
Turned pale as the snow
And started to go
Saying what is the use
When a maid of sixteen
Would lay down her life
For white, orange, and green."

His singing was interrupted by the old farmer explaining that he had to get back to his wife as it was getting a bit late. He held his thumb up in the air and shouted, "Up the IRA!" and left.

"Steven, I think I'll get some sleep now as I stayed up readin' last night. We'd best get back to our lads tomorrow."

Aye, but I'm not sleepy at all. I think I'll find out what happened to Brian out West and see how he got back to Ireland."

"Aye, and fill me in at daybreak as we're walkin' back to Newton-Hamilton." Steven started reading the next entry

dated September, 1852 at Fort Laramie. A soft breeze brushed through the white heather outside the shed. All of Northern Ireland seemed to glow in luminescence. Steven became so absorbed in his reading that he didn't know if he was in Ireland or the far West.

CHAPTER VIII

A Windy, Dusty, Western Fort

Brian lay there on his bunk at midnight looking out of the barrack windows at the stars and moon. The wind whistled past the rustic buildings of Fort Laramie in the Dakota Territory. Here he was, a member of Company G of the Mounted Rifles. He had gone through six months of rugged training back in Virginia and had ridden on horse-back all the way from Fort Kearney, Nebraska, his first post.

He couldn't believe the dull grey monotony and stupidity of basic military training in Virginia. How many times that harsh sounding reveille bugle sounded! Everything had to be on a schedule, march to the food hall at sunrise. March to the drill grounds by 7 a.m. Clean rifles at 8 a.m. And the boring talks by bloated officers on killing a savage enemy, the American Indian. Then they would march to the food hall again at high noon. After lunch it was "ready, mount," "ready, dismount," on shaggy brown training horses. Then by mid afternoon it was marching again on the drill grounds. By sunset we would march to the food hall again. Evenings were spent scrubbing down the barracks for inspection. Did it ever rain down there! You'd think we were in the clouds themselves when it thundered. The rain made Brian's stirrup-bent knees ache with pain.

God, how he remembered those imbecilic company commanders chewing tobacco, and blaring out orders and inspecting the soldiers' faces to see if they were really clean shaven. After months of this ridiculous routine following a tight schedule, he was more than ready for a western post. Schedules—why schedules? We never had such a thing in Ireland, but everybody went by the sun. When winter came and there were only five or six hours of daylight, we'd work in fields only that amount of time and sleep late in the mornings. In summer, when the day was twenty hours long, we'd work out in the fields a brave long while. But to maintain a fixed schedule no matter what time of year it is, is nothing more than forced insanity! Perhaps he should have returned to Ireland and not listened to old Sam Brady about going out West. Sam was dead now so what did it matter?

All that he could remember coming West was the ever-widening horizon and the ever-brightening sun. Groves of cottonwood trees gave way to open prairies now brown with the approaching autumn. At sunset, a few hours before he turned in, he watched glowing Laramie Peak redden in silence. This country was so open and stark and vast it was like nothing he could have expected on the same planet that houses Ireland. Yet it reminded him of some of the barren hill country in western Cavan where there were no houses or people. The day he arrived at Fort Laramie he stopped in a windy valley some two hours before the fort. Jack pines clung to the grassy hills and wind constantly brushed through their needles. He had never experienced such a strong sun in a stark blue sky. That valley seemed to have a presence in it that he couldn't explain. He felt something there; perhaps those bending jack pines gave it voice. As he approached the distant fort, there was no full moon bigger than that Dakota moon looming up over prairie mounds.

Sam had died just thirty days before Brian left for Virginia. In June, 1851, a rail slipped off the top of a pile and crushed the old, toothless Irishman to death. Many a night in those Virginia swamplands where so many black people dwelt, Brian thought of Sam. It was quite a blow to him losing yet another close friend. He missed hearing about the crazy cousin of his back in Dublin. He missed Sam's fatherly advice about Teresa or about going West and seeing America. First his mother, then his father, then Peter and Iguk and now Sam Brady. Yes, Sam had helped him understand himself and America a little better. It was Sam who gave him an interest in plants and trees. He had told him that some trees were sacred according to his Druid ancestors. One particular tree back in County Monaghan was sacred to Sam. It was an old Holm oak tree near Loch Mucknoe. From the time Sam was a boy until he left Ireland, he made wishes at the foot of that tree. While Peter had taught him an appreciation for poetry (perhaps, someday he would write a poem), Sam had taught him respect for the vegetable mold of our green planet. Sam's death killed part of Brian, but Sam's life got him to Fort Laramie.

Brian lingered on with the railroad until December, joined the Army with hopes of going West and endured the humiliation of basic training south of Washington, D.C. To his joy, he was sent West to Fort Kearney and after three months of listless duty was transferred to Fort Laramie beneath distant Laramie Peak and by the junction of the Laramie and North Platte Rivers. He was given to understand that Fort Laramie served an important strategic role in the western settlement of this nation. Thousands of emigrants passed by the fort en route to Utah, Oregon, and California. The Indians of the area were supposedly peaceful and resigned to the inevitable spread of white civilization. Just in case they changed their minds, there was Fort Laramie.

Brian was one of 113 men stationed at the fort. His commanding officer was Captain Garnett and his company commander was a fellow Irishman by the name of Lieutenant James Shaughnessy from County Clare south of Cavan.

One hour before sunrise, Brian awakened to the blare of a reveille bugle. Mist hugged the surface of the North Platte River and its bordering cottonwood trees as Brian quickly dressed and fell into formation out on the dusty drill field beneath rolling prairie mounds with cawing crows.

"Ah right you soldiers. Today yar goin' on a bivouac in the Black Hills.* There's been smoke signals from atop Laramie Peak last evenin' and we gotta see what's what. Them savages think that bleak old mountain is holy or somethin'. Now get over to the mess hall and have a solid breakfast." Lieutenant Shaughnessy spoke with a gruff voice and with a big cigar in the corner of his mouth.

"Private McBride, hold up a minute," Shaughnessy snapped.

"Yes sir," he sounded back.

"I hear yar from Ireland. What part?"

"County Cavan."

"Were ya there durin' the famine?"

"Aye, 'twas shockin' bad times. Me father and mother died, sir."

"Well, you'll be feelin' at home out here, lad. Hundreds have died of Asiatic Cholera in the few years past. They say there's one grave a mile from Westport Landing to Laramie and that's over six hundred miles."

"Oh aye, I've heard tell of the cholera. It's affected mostly emigrants hasn't it sir?"

"Yes, lad and Injuns. Wisht it killed off more injuns than whites, but that's not the case. This here injun duty is quiet— not like the Mexican Wars I fought in a few years back— plenty of action there. But go on now, have yar breakfast."

"Yes, sir. They talked of the Mexican Wars in Boston, I recall."

"Aye, I suppose they did."

After a hot breakfast prepared by an old Negro cook who kept staring at Brian, the troopers fell into formation, saddled up their horses brought out from the stables and mounted. Brian had to carry the colors of "Company G,"

---

* The Laramie range was considered to be part of the Black Hills during the nineteenth century.

and a handful of people waved goodbye as they left the gates of the fort and rode out into sagebrush and rolling dry prairie. Laramie Peak loomed to the West rising straight up like a blue pyramid. After nearly a full day's ride, they entered a scrub pine forest and climbed into warm and sunny foothills. One glittering ponderosa pine hissed in the wind with all of its glowing needles reflecting brilliant light. This is strange country, Brian thought. He shaded his eyes from the painful glare of the sun as the two columns of troopers slowly wound their way up rocky slopes.

Brian couldn't help but notice that the men who had been stationed out here for over a year were quite tan—almost too tan to be white men.

"Where ya from, pardner," asked a blond-haired trooper.

"County Cavan, Ireland."

"Man, I thought I was a long ways from home. I'm from Canton, Ohio."

"Is that anywhere near Niagara falls?"

"Naw. But I seen 'em. They're mighty big and misty."

"Aye, I can imagine standin' there and feelin' like some wee insect or somethin'."

"Naw. They make me feel big, as big as America itself."

"You Americans have things big, don't yous."

"You said it, pardner."

Lieutenant Shaughnessy blared out, "Ready, halt. Dismount."

They all took out some beef jerky from their saddle bags and drank swigs of canteen water. A grove of quaking aspen above them had turned to a brilliant autumnal gold under deep blue, cloudless skies. Leaves trembled with each breeze.

"This is some country," Brian remarked to his Ohio friend.

"Yep, and it's all ours."

"Ours? Meaning who?"

"Americans, who else?"

"I suppose I better not ask who Americans are?"

"Man, you and me, that's who."

Brian remained silent because he didn't want to get into an argument. He felt like asking if Iguk or the Sioux Indians camped near the fort were Americans.

"Aw, I know why yer askin' them dumb questions. Because yer Irish and wonderin' if yer American yet, hunh?"

"Aye, I guess that's it."

"Yer in the best damned army in the world, so it makes you American, right?"

"Aye."

"Ready, mount!" commanded the lieutenant.

They proceeded toward the base of Laramie Peak and looked up at the miles of rocky shelves and dense stands of spruce and fir. One big cumulus cloud hovered over the pointed summit of the mountain. The air was bracing and fragrant. The going became tedious and loose rocks constantly rolled down from the upper end of the column of troopers to the lower. The horses wheezed and coughed.

"Ready, dismount!" commanded Shaughnessy.

They led their horses by the reins up impossibly steep and rocky terrain. They set up camp for the night and welcomed the warmth of their bedrolls in the chilly air. The soldiers stared up at the flickering stars in a black sky. Someone played lonesome tunes on a harmonica to keep the first watch company. Brian had no trouble sleeping in that crisp mountain air. Here he slept some nine thousand feet above his old Irish home.

"Private McBride, Private Smith, Private Williams and Private Arthur, proceed up the slope to the summit and take any necessary action against the smoke signalers," Shaughnessy ordered in a low voice early the next morning. The four of them grabbed something to eat and climbed up sheer granite cliffs to the summit as quietly as they could in the morning sun. Fortunately for them a stiff wind at the summit concealed the noise of their stumbling boots. Brian cleared the last cliff first and stared out into the vast eastern prairies. He thought he could make out the smoke curling up from Fort Laramie and reflected that these Indians should have investigated the soldiers' smoke as well. The spiney ridge above them looked like the back of an immense stegosaurus.

"Brian, get down, don't you see 'em," shouted Private Smith, the blond-haired trooper from Canton, Ohio. Private Arthur raised his pistol, aimed and fired at an old Shoshone Indian who fell to the ground. At the same time Private Williams fired at two other unarmed Indians and killed them instantly with blood oozing out of their necks and chests.

"We did it! We did it! Hooray for Company G!" shouted Private Smith.

Brian was shocked if not horrified. Just then they heard the patter of drums from a valley below, and they saw a ring of distant tipis in a valley opposite the rest of their company. The troopers raced down the summit almost breaking their necks. Brian slipped and stumbled into a rocky den and all of the sudden felt a thousand needles strike his shin bone. The other soldiers pounced on a black and yellow rattlesnake and crushed its bony little skull and dragged Brian out of there. Everything became whoozy, and he passed out.

The next evening Mrs. Shaughnessy, the lieutenant's sassy Texas bride, cared for Brian, patting his forehead with damp cloths and changing his dressing over the snake bite which had been slashed open with a sharp knife back at Laramie Peak.

"Where am I, mame?"

"Back at the fort, trooper. You did a fayne job killing those Indians!" said Mrs. Shaughnessy, a thirty-five year old woman with blond hair streaked with grey.

"Ah, sure them Indians was harmless. That's why the Lord punished me as I stood by and did nothing."

"What kind of talk is that, now, coming from an American soldier," she said in a surprised tone.

"Them Indians is American, too, aren't they?"

"Well, I suppose they are, but . . . I mean . . . well, my husband thinks they're our enemy and . . . "

"What do *you* think, Mrs. Shaughnessy?"

She secretly admired his vitality.

"I think what my husband thinks!"

"Because he's yer husband, or because you agree with him?"

"Well because . . . both! Here, let me change that cloth."

Brian attempted to move his leg, but it weighed a ton. He thought of Teresa. If only he had Teresa here. Why didn't she send answers through Elish? Sure, his handwriting was bad, but Elish must be able to read it to Teresa alright.

"You're delirious, that's why you're talking so funny."

"Aye, it's delirious I am."

"Well, my husband's off on another bivouac. I think Company C and G are out this time. He has taken a liking to you because youh from his old country. I guess he likes your spunk. . . . "

Brian fell asleep while Mrs. Shaughnessy cared for her baby in the next room.

"Here, have some broth. It will do you good," said Sandy Shaughnessy bending over Brian. He could see the bases of her big breasts.

"Are you feeling stronger?" she asked.

"Aye, a bit. But me leg is as stiff as a board."

"Oh," she said patting his forehead. "Stiff as a bowd, hunh." She winked at him and got up to take a boiling bottle off a wood stove.

"Tell me, Brian. Do you have a sweetheart?"

"Ah no. I met a pretty girl back in Canada, but . . . "

"You didn't have her, eh?"

Brian's face flushed, and he didn't answer.

"It's nothing to be ashamed of Brian, is it now?"

Her baby started crying in the next room. She went and got it and brought it into Brian's room by his bedside.

"Sarah, this here is Brian McBride, wouldn't you like to have a man like that as your husband someday?"

"Ah, Mrs. Shaughnessy, don't be talking that way now."

"Sandy, call me Sandy," she said leaning over Brian with her plunging neckline plunging into his eyes.

"About them Indians. Ya still think they ain't Americans?"

"Brian, Indians are whatever you think they are. As for me . . . the Sioux aren't that bad, I guess. But they do have ignorant habits."

"Why should we be killing them?"

"Stop asking questions. You'll go crazy. Are you going crazy?" she said as she rubbed a breast against his arm.

"Look at Sarah, now. If ya don't mind me sayin' so . . . "

"You'd like to reserve her for your wife."

"Ah, no. I was goin' to say . . . "

"You don't have to wait that long . . . "

"I was goin' to say Sarah's a pretty dark girl for a white baby."

"What are you saying," Sandy asked in anger. "Are you implying I had an affair with a dirty Indian?"

"No, no, not at all. I'm sayin' that I noticed people who've been out here a while are darker than people, say, in Ireland. And that baby of yours . . . well . . . what I'm tryin' to say is . . . is the land out here seems to be turning whites into reds."

"You're delirious. Delirious and out of your mind."

"Listen, if whites turn into Indians out here over the

years, we'll not be fighting Indians will we? We'd be fighting ourselves."

"Whites will stay white! Races don't change!" Sandy huffed out of the room and slammed the door.

A week later, Brian hobbled around on the drill field and took gruff orders from Lieutenant Shaughnessy. He had fallen out of favor with the officer and was given the worst work detail each day at the rubbish heaps. The old black cook couldn't help but notice there was a second nigger at the fort, only this one was white. They both spoke with strange accents and both had different manners.

War drums thumped in the distance as trouble brewed at the nearby North Platte ferry. A band of Shoshone Indians who had been attacked back at Laramie Peak had seized the boat and not permitted any emigrants to cross the river. They complained that no matter how peaceful they remained, white men kept building new forts, blazing new trails across their hunting lands, and killing, by piecemeal, their oldest and most respected warriors. The whites had no respect for sacred mountains. Lord knows what will become of the Black Hills. That evening the wind blew hard, and dry September dust collected in ripples over the porch of the barracks. Coyotes howled in the pale moonlight. Brian felt lonesome, very lonesome.

Company C was called again to take care of the Indian trouble. Brian no longer carrying the troop colors, was at the rear of the column as the soldiers rode out of the fort toward the seized ferry boat.

"Draw sabers!" commanded Shaughnessy.

As men drew near the Indians, their sabers flashing in the sunlight, a chief whose name was Washakie raised his hand. The lieutenant raised his.

"Get yar scoundrels out of here or you die!" Shaughnessy ordered.

"Listen to our grievances," the chief replied.

"Grievances, hell! Go live with the other animals of the

woods and leave us to running things around here."

"You have let too many people cross our land. Forty-thousand people this year past. Enough is enough!"

"You are enough, I say," Shaughnessy quipped with a reddened face. "Just who the hell do you think you are bird brain?"

"Your national symbol is the eagle, is it not?"

"Don't get smart with me you savage bastard. I'll ram this saber down yar throat."

Chief Washakie ordered his Indians to stand firm:

"Be careful of the dust you throw when you are not sure of the wind."

"That does it," Shaughnessy roared.

The lieutenant chomped on his cigar and commanded, "Ready, charge!" The troopers charged full fury into the band of Shoshone and slashed furiously to the left and right. Chief Washakie and his followers retreated leaving nine slaughtered brethren behind. One dying Indian was shot in the head to relieve his suffering. Brian had to dismount by a sagebrush so he could vomit as the wailing Indians rode off in the distance. That night the troopers chewed tobacco and played poker while Brian took a walk by himself. One of the card players, spitting some tobacco, said,

"We sure caught 'em that time, didn't we boys?"

"Yeap, those bastards won't seize no ferry boat now, unless it's in hell."

They roared with laughter. Brian heard the laughter and wished that he was back on the Fitchburg line or even in the North Square slums, certainly on Simon's farm, most assuredly in Dublin with Teresa. How is it that my close friends cause me to get farther and farther away from Ireland? The wind and coyotes howled and stars looked like shattered pieces of glass. He saw the old Negro cook dumping some garbage in a pit not far from Old Bedlam, the officer's quarters, and he ambled up to him:

"Joe, how is it with you?" Brian asked in a melancholic tone.

"Reckon as well as the Lord will permit."

"That's a good way of puttin' it, Joe."

"You Irish and us black folk got somepin' in common—sufferin' boy, sufferin'. You'd best watch yoself, boy—cause people round heah knows you ain't happy with the way things is a-goin'. Boy, when I sees you in da mess hall, I *knows* things ain't right fo' you."

"What do ya mean, Joe?"

"Jist that, boy, jist that. If I was you, I think I'd cut out a heah."

"Why haven't you done the same?"

"What's a runaway nigga good fo' in America, hunh? I knows fo' I'm from South Carolina. I could sho' yoo whippin' scars that'd make yoo sick."

"I reckon you know what sufferin' is alright," Brian said trying to imitate his expression.

"Well, there yoo have it. Hush, now, boy, an officer's a-comin'."

"Private McBride, get back to the barracks and stay put until someone calls for you tomorrow to see Captain Garnett," ordered a lieutenant.

Brian trudged back to his bunk and endured the sounds of a poker game until midnight. The troopers roared with laughter over stupid jokes. Had Brian lived in another era he would have felt they weren't unlike the storm troopers of World War II in occupied France or Holland. At three in the morning someone tapped on his window. He awakened, looked out and saw old Joe holding the reins of a horse. He quickly dressed and went out.

"Boy, you'd better git, now, git. Yoo knows yoo in trouble if the Captain wants to see yoo."

The Irish lad shook hands with his black friend, mounted the horse and rode off quietly toward the sacred Black Hills.

He threw away his trooper's hat and kerchief and kicked the horse into a galloping gait. By George, good old Joe had packed his saddlebags with several days' rations! He won't get caught, Brian rationalized. Sure he won't. If he does, I'll come back here with a bunch of Indians and save him.

Steven, the IRA rebel, mumbled to himself in the darkness of an Irish night, *"If I'd been in that kind of army, I'd quit, too. They were a bunch of Tommies trying to impose their ways on a different people."* Michael tossed in his sleep and seemed to be mumbling something, but Steven couldn't make it out.

Brian used up his precious food supply in crossing the vast stretches of open prairie and desert dotted with distant antelope and buffalo. He thought he saw a large grey buffalo, but he wasn't sure. Maybe his eyes were playing tricks on him. For several nights he slept by a lonesome prairie fire wondering if the troopers would catch up. When thoughts of Ireland drifted into his mind he contemplated suicide. Why in God's name had he come so far from his native land, from his sister, from his fellow Irishmen? Peter Flanigan and Sam Brady must have been agents of the devil. Here he was, a deserter, by himself in the middle of the most unearthly land studded with cactus. He had circled far away from Fort Caspar, farther up on the Platte and crossed the river several miles south. He didn't want to encounter more troopers under the slopes of Caspar Mountain. What was all this for? His life was turning into a hellish nightmare. Brian learned to tolerate the gummy taste of the inside of cactus and the strong carrot taste of yucca roots. He looked off in the distance one morning to see floating white clouds, or were they mountains? He wasn't sure. Perhaps he was crazy from too much yucca root. He saddled up and, as he slowly approached that distant floating whiteness, he saw that those clouds had become mountains. They beckoned him to come. "I will look unto the mountains whence cometh my strength," he thought to himself. They drew him like magnets, and, after two more days of fast riding having only water for nourishment, Brian entered the early September woodlands of the Wind River Mountains of Wyoming. He had come by way of Hell's half acre and the Big Horn River flowing toward the country of bubbling springs.

Brian satisfied his hunger with mountain berries and a trout that he managed to hit with a rock in shallow water. The famine days in Ireland paid off in enabling him to withstand days of hunger. Naturally he thought nothing of eating a fresh raw fish. A jagged, icy peak loomed high above him in the setting sun and he thought to himself: "If I can climb that mountain, my life has meaning," he wagered to himself. "If I die . . . well . . . I die five thousand miles from home."

Brian began plodding his way through darkening forests of spruce and fir. At first his breathing seemed very heavy, and the quiet night atmosphere accentuated his huffing and puffing. But his lungs gradually grew accustomed to the task of breathing at an altitude ten thousand feet higher than County Cavan. The higher he got, the cooler the air became. The very sound of a rushing alpine brook tumbling over glacial boulders made him shiver. He sat down by a waterfall for a rest and heard the pipping of a striped ground squirrel. The ice cold water refreshed him, even hurt his teeth, while a bright, full moon glowed through creaking branches of spruces which barely concealed lofty, luminous peaks high above. He began to believe that he was in his afterlife.

He got up and continued his trek toward a glowing icy summit. Gnarled, twisted limber pine, crinkly monument plant, and dwarf willows were like nothing back in Ireland. Dense, matted tundra coated the rocky soil, giving the evening landscape an appearance of giant, ruffled carpet leading to God knows where. In the pitch darkenss of midnight, Brian staggered over loose rocks of an immense boulder field just above the timberline. Then he saw his destination, an immensely jagged peak flanked by strips of icy snow glowing with iridescence in the moonbeams.

After much struggle, he reached an upper ledge and stared down into a chasm two thousand feet below. Shimmering, pulsating threads of Northern Lights laced the black sky. Brian wormed his way up a narrow chimney in a granite cliff. Several times he lost his footing but managed to claw his way back up. Then a sloping ice field hindered his progress. However, Brian gingerly stepped across the slippery ice until he arrived at the base of a jagged, windy wall of rock. After an hour or so of struggling up a pitted, grooved face of rock, he elbowed his way to a tiny summit no larger than his father's small room. He ate some snow, stretched out on a boulder and fell asleep under brilliant stars looking more like discs than pinpoints.

At dawn he awakened himself with his own shivering. God it was cold. A faint reddish hue filled the frosty air. The dull, brown desert far below gradually assumed a more realistic appearance. As the sun bobbed up over the rim of the planet, Brian squinted like a bat at midday. The whole Wind River Range glowed in a golden light, while the narrow valleys far below remained dim and grey. Despite his hunger, Brian felt like a celtic warrior from ancient times as the shadow of his mountain spread far to the West. He stood and stared into a universe of space for an hour or more until he heard distant drums thumping like dinosaur hearts. Somewhere far below him were his friends, the Indians. He knew he must return to the valleys to join them.

CHAPTER IX

The Indian Connection

By the time Brian had made his tiring descent into the foothill country, snow began to fly. At first it had gathered in wisps out on the rocky promontories; then it collected in circles around the twisted silver trunks of limber pines. The sky had become grey and fuzzy, and only dim shadows cast themselves on the forest floor. Brian, having only a trooper's dress jacket and no hat, was miserably cold, but his continual movement kept him from freezing. This is a bad as livin' in a ditch, he thought to himself. In fact, it was worse. He must return to his native land and put on a different uniform, a rebel's uniform to fight for Irish freedom.

"Now yer talkin', lad!" Steven said out loud in the cowshed beneath Slieve Gullion. Michael groaned in his sleep with Irish moonbeams flowing across his face. Steven knew that tomorrow would bring a fight, perhaps his most spirited one since joining the IRA.

Brian trudged through foot-deep snow wondering where in God's name he could go.

"What happened to them drums?" he shouted in a dark jack pine forest. Just then he felt an iron grip on his arm. He quickly confronted a dark face and black eyes of a fierce looking Shoshone warrior:

"Neh—Goochoo—doah! Unuh?"

"I don't understand. Do you speak English?"

The warrior pointed to himself and repeated, "Neh," and then he said slowly, "Goochoo—doah." He pointed to Brian and asked, "Unuh?"

Brian thought to himself, here we go again, just like Canada all over. He pointed to himself and said, "Me . . . Brian McBride . . . from . . . ," and he looked way off in the distance, ". . . Ireland." The Indian gave the faintest trace of a smile and pointed to himself, "Goo-choo-doah!"

"Aye, yer name is Goo-chew-doah!"

The young Indian led him through the jack pines for a mile or so, and they arrived at a ring of white tepees with smoke curling out of their pointed tops passing through ghostly branches of dead trees. One Indian sat at a blazing fire smoking a long pipe. When Brian approached him, he saw that it was English speaking Chief Washakie whom he had seen back at Fort Laramie.

"I see you are a deserter," the chief said sternly.

"Yes, I'm a deserter, indeed."

"You are not American from the way you talk."

"Indeed I'm not. I'm from Ireland."

"Ayeland is where?"

"Across the sea."

"Oh, where the big owl goes, yes. Why did you desert?"

"Well now, ta put it bluntly, I didn't like what the bloody blokes was doin' to yous. What big owl?"

"Blokes? Big owl that fly our ancestor across seas. He have find his way back here. But what are blokes?"

"Troopers."

"You disapprove of what troopers do to Indians, why?"

Brian proceeded to explain his anti-British feelings and told Washakie of the famine in Ireland while England stood by empty handed to watch countless thousands of Irish die of starvation and disease.

"Irishman, you are in America, though, and Americans

aren't the British are they? How I know you not spy? You look like spy!"

Brian was thunderstruck with this accusation. Perhaps Chief Washakie felt that Brian's anger and mystification were signs of his guilt and therefore ordered Brian thrown into a hunger cave high above the rapids of the Popo Agie River. He was to exist in that cave for two agonizing weeks. They led him over rocky terrain studded with yucca and sagebrush high over the rapids of the Popo Agie. Several twisted cottonwood trees lay beneath him in a narrow, winding valley which led up to higher, open fields at the base of the Wind River Mountains. A slight mist rose from the rushing waters below. After they climbed down a steep, red sandstone cliff, they approached a small cave about twenty feet deep with a narrow entrance. They pushed him into the cave and placed a heavy, think sandstone slab over the mouth of the cave and piled rocks in front of the slab. Only a narrow slit of sunlight threaded into an otherwise black void.

Brian moaned a little wondering if he was going to die here. He wondered why Washakie did not believe him. Washakie had honest, thoughtful eyes; why was he doing this? Brian looked at the slit of sunlight and followed it to where it lit on the dark wall of the cave. He saw a few black ants crawling along the wall, and he ate them. But wait a minute, was he seeing things? A strange form was carved into the wall with tentacles coming out of his head, deep, deep eye sockets, two slits for nostrils and a thin, curving mouth. It seemed to stare hideously at Brian, and it made him feel slightly queasy. As the sun sank in the sky that thin beam changed its angle until it disappeared altogether. He just couldn't fathom why the Indians would put him in this black pit.

"Where shall I sleep in this wee hole," Brian said aloud. His voice echoed as though he were in a marble tomb. He felt some feathers and rabbit fur, probably the remains of an old coyote den, and stretched out as best he could. Just as he was about to doze off to the Dublin of his dreams, he felt a stinging bite on the back of his neck. He slapped his neck with all his might to see the gooshy remains of a black spider in his fingers. God that bite stung! Moments later he felt a terrible nausea and a splitting headache. Sweat broke out on his forehead. Now he knew what Peter Flanigan must have gone through aboard the *Pinzance*. In his delirium mixed visions whirled through his brain: first Ireland, then Fort Laramie, then the swamps of Virginia, then Boston. Everything whirled around like a giant whirlpool of color and memories.

"Brian, give me a hand, would ya," asked his father. "If we're gona take this here sow ta market, I'll be needin' yer help."

"Aye, father, I'm comin'."

That horribly ugly sow we had back before the famine came to mind. She was a big pig with huge tusks coming out of the sides of her snout, and she grunted with deep chest tones like some sort of prehistoric monster.

"Brian, you grab hold of her tail, and I'll try to put a rope around her neck."

"God, if she doesn't smell somethin' terrible, father. Are ya sure we have ta take this one ta market?"

"Aye, indeed we do."

Just as father was about to put a rope around her neck, the sow charged him wagging her head back and forth like a jungle beast. She grabbed hold of father's fingers and started tearing away. Blood spurted all over the grass outside the pigshed. God, I thought he lost his fingers, but he pulled away his hand quickly enough to save them. Brian thought to himself that their dog Patch finished the job on his father's fingers. As he was trying to think whatever became of that ugly sow, the old black cook at Fort Laramie shouted for help.

"Where are you," Brian shouted back.

"Oveh heah."

Brian looked through the mist of a swamp. Where was he? In

Virginia? He walked out of the training camp into the damp, misty air of the Virginia swamplands. Whipporwills whistled in the distance, and an eery, green moon rose above the tulip trees.

"Where are you?" he shouted again.

Then he saw the Negro cook chained to a pine tree with whip lashings cut deep into his back. He was unconscious. Brian cupped his hands to a stream and brought the Negro some water to revive him.

"Son, you a good ole boy ta help dis here nigger. I done run away frum da pecan plantation in South Carolina. And dey caughts up wid me."

"Here, let me break that chain," Brian said.

"No man heah on earth kin break dat chain but me, son."

The black man became dark mist hovering above an Arctic glacier. Winds howled furiously through scrubby spruce on a cliff overlooking the frozen sea. Just a sliver of a moon peaked above the endless grey horizons of ice floes, and hard, cold islands with scrubby willows.

"Is that you, Iguk," Brian shouted.

"Eyes, you good to see me coming from so far. Just come back from Ellesmere Island with five seal on my dogsled."

"Did you get to Ottawa, Iguk?"

"Have not gone yet. How you know I want to go?"

Iguk raced past Brian headed for the moon like shamans of yore. Brian shivered in his Irish sweater, or was it his U.S. Calvary jacket? But wait, what happened to the ice floes? He rolled over in the dark and bumped his head on a rocky projection in the cave where the sun glimmered in on a narrow beam lighting up that carving in the wall. How long he had been asleep, he did not know—perhaps a day—perhaps two or three. He still had a fever but felt pangs of hunger and thirst. God he was hungry. He licked the moist walls of the cave deriving some satisfaction, but not much as he heard the roar of the clear, cold Popo Agie not more than a hundred yards away. Brian tried to push out the sandstone slab at the cave's entrance, but he failed. He stared at the carving or petroglyph to see that its mouth wasn't curving but straight. Had it changed? He crawled up to it and counted its stick-like fingers raised up to either side of its head. Five and five make ten. At least he's human, whatever else he is. Brian heard something scuttle on the cave floor and then heard a chirping sound. He crawled closer to the sound and faintly saw a black grasshopper huddled in some white rabbit fur. He seized the insect and devoured it raw licking his lips and delighting in the nut-like flavor in his mouth.

He crawled back to his primitive bed and lay thinking a while before his fever rose and he fell off into unconsciousness. Did he get up in his sleep and find another grasshopper to eat, or was he dreaming?

"Please, Mister Flanigan, no more," a schoolboy shouted.

"I'm following Killeshandra's school code, me boy. You cheated on your exam and need a wee whipping for the likes of that."

The boy screamed piercing Peter Flanigan's soul. He coughed and returned to his desk while the blond-haired boy sobbed and went back to his writing table. Peter just stared out of the window at the green and rolling countryside of County Cavan with rows of potato and barley fields. He thought to himself that the Lord above will punish him and his fellow man for following letters of the law which violate the inner spirit. Peter Flanigan sat at his desk failing to respond to his pupil's questions.

"Mr. Flanigan, which river is larger, the Danube or the Saint Lawrence? Mr. Flanigan . . . "

"Irishman! Irishman, get up, get up my son," demanded Chief Washakie standing in the brilliant sunlight in front of Brian. Brian staggered to his feet and fell down again asking the chief why he had put him through all this torture.

"We have a faction in our tribe, Irishman. Years back, our beloved Sacajawea left us to help white men. She help them find passage to the big water to the West. Ever since then, many Shoshone people believe we dare not help white men again because it mean even more white men come from East."

"Oh, aye. But surely ya don't think I'll . . . "

"I for many days worried about you, but know Great Spirit will show us truth about you by letting you live. How did he make time pass for you?"

"That's a strange way a puttin' it. But time passed for me, aye, it did indeed. Maybe it was that strange carving on the wall of the cave that did it."

"Great Spirit make that man. He change every time I go there. Sometime he have five fingers on each hand, sometime six. He change like the sky. He is presence of something bigger than you or me."

"Would he bite me? Something did!"

"Do not know, but if he bite it is to give you vision."

"Aye."

"You see vision?"

"Aye, but they were all mixed. I don't remember them rightly."

Brian felt faint from hunger and nearly collapsed after the chief had lifted him up to support him. They inched slowly toward the river bed and two horses which would carry them back to camp. Brian couldn't help but sense Washakie's concern and friendship.

"Before we ride back, take long drink from Popo Agie and then wash off. See the berries along the shoreline? Have some. You eat big back at camp."

Brian flopped down in the river and sipped, then gulped the icy, clear water. He grabbed a few dark, sour chokecherries and swallowed them whole. Already he felt a little stronger as he was helped up onto his horse. In just a little while they approached a ring of white tepees and dismounted.

"Sit and smoke at the pipe of peace."

Washakie showed Brian the ritualistic manner of smoking by

first holding the pipe up to each of the four cardinal directions. The peace pipe had a buffalo carved on it pointing toward the smoker.

"What do you intend to do Irishman? Go back to Ireland?"

"Well, yes, I s'pose I will, but I'd like to stay with you people a while until Fort Laramie thinks I'm dead or somethin'. Unless you plan on throwing me back in that cave."

Washakie chuckled and replied, "Good idea to stay with us. Winter comes and you will want to stay with us until spring when we will show you the way to Grandmother's Land."

"Grandmother's Land? Oh aye, that's what Iguk said, too, I think."

"Iguk?"

"An Eskimo friend of mine I met on the Saint Lawrence River."

"Eskimo? What is meaning of Eskimo?"

"Natives from the far North, Baffinland if I remember correctly. They harpoon seals and ride on dogsleds."

"Seals? This must be animals. Yes, my son. Yes, you may stay with us until the grass grows green. My people trust you since you lived in cave."

"I'm not a hunter but a farmer. But I'll be happy to help yous in any way I'm able."

"Fight troopers if necessary?"

"Aye, I'd fight them bastards if I had to!"

"Good, my son, good. You even say this after the hunger cave."

"I saw what they did to you at the North Platte Ferry, and it made me sick."

"You were there? Did you kill any of my men?" Washakie asked showing signs of doubt again.

"I was too busy vomitin' to do any fightin'."

100

"You were sick from fear or from . . . "

"Not fear, from disgust!"

"Yes, I believe you, Irishman."

Brian was led into a tepee and given warm furs to wear and some hot pemmican cakes of pounded meat and berries. He ate ravenously, after two weeks of eating only insects. Then he was given a bowl of hot tea which tasted like the woodlands he had been through, wild and ambrosial. Washakie saw that Brian fought sleep and pointed to a buffalo robe for a bed. He soon passed out dreaming of more pleasant things back in pre-famine Ireland.

As he gradually woke up the next morning, he sensed a pair of eyes staring at him. When his vision came into focus, he saw a slender, not overly pretty, dark-haired maiden smiling at him saying in a rich tone of voice,

"Me Chilsipee, you Brian?"

"Chilsipee? A beautiful name, Chilsipee."

"Brian, I given as your woman."

"Married ya mean? You have been given to me in marriage?"

"Yes, chief give me you."

"Chilsipee, it's not that I don't like you . . . yer . . . a fine woman . . . but . . . "

As he said "But," she disrobed exposing her warm brown body with small but firm breasts and she held out her arms for him to come. He wasn't going to resist this time. If Chilsipee was given to him by the chief, well then, why shouldn't he have her? She crawled into his buffalo robe bed, and they made love during most of the morning until their hunger disturbed them. This was Brian's first sexual love, and it was thoroughly satisfying to him. By the end of the day he had fallen in love with his warm Chilsipee. He liked her tone of voice, the depth of her eyes, and her genuine desire to please him and learn about him and his homeland. By midnight, in-between their lovemaking, Brian had told

101

her many of the details of his native County Cavan, the famine, Dublin and its wretched soup kitchen, Teresa, Peter Flanigan, and the voyage across the Atlantic, Quebec, North Square, the Walden Woods, Fort Laramie, and the hunger cave. Her solution to his tragedy and sorrow was to love him, and his release from the strain of heavy memories was to love her.

By the second morning in the tepee, they were both hungry and came out into the sun. Chief Washakie welcomed them and asked Brian if he would care to leave his woman a few days to help with a buffalo hunt. Chilsipee nodded, and Brian agreed to go when he had eaten a native American breakfast of chokecherry gravy, gooseberries, and sage grouse. Chilsipee had gathered many baskets of berries during September. They were still plump and juicy for Ye bawne or autumn.

The band of Shoshones with their white orphan filed out of the Wind Rivers and headed East toward the Powder River. Brian was dressed in buckskins and mocassins, a far more comfortable dress than any army uniform. By now he was bearded and quite tan. He had been given a rifle and was to be their cover man. In the distance they saw a white wagon train headed West toward California. When they got to within a half mile of the whites, the ground before them was pelted with rifle fire. Fortunately, no one was hit. Goo-choo-doah, the man who captured Brian weeks earlier, let out a war whoop, and the whites fired another round of shots at them, but they were out of range. Then came hours and hours of peace where the prairie grasses talked to them. Brian felt that if "Americans" were ever to become *Americans*, they would have to learn how to listen to prairie grass as the Shoshones did. By the end of the day, a brave having the name Dorsawee went ahead to scout for buffalo in the next valley. He came back to report the presence of a herd of over one hundred grazing in tall grass.

Several Indians rode up into the herd reddened by a glowing sunset and killed five or six animals with their bow and arrows. Everytime an arrow thunked home, Brian knew a

102

buffalo had been fatally wounded. The men butchered the animals and skinned them. Brian was told that the buffalo was the mainstay of their tribe. They ate its meat, used its furs for warmth, its tail for a fly swatter, its bones for soup ladles, its skull for ceremonial dances, and its horns for headdress. It was as useful to the Indians as the potato to the Irishman, and if the supply of these natural commodities ever dwindled, so did the population of these two aboriginal races of people.

After a big prairie roast of fresh buffalo steaks, the band of Indians spread around the campfire in a circle and told tales in Shoshone. All laughed but Brian who simply stared at the vast spaces of Wyoming and thought of his Chilsipee and her warm body. Only when he fantasized about her, could he begin to close his eyes. It was funny how much he needed her after his womanless life before. Sensing that Brian was not with them, Chief Washakie told a strange tale for the benefit of Brian in English:

"An Indian from the far northlands, having lost a sister whom he loved very much, resolved to seek her and made twelve days' travel toward the setting sun without eating or drinking; at the end of which his sister appeared to him at evening, with a plate of meal cooked with water."

Brian's thoughts wandered back to living in a ditch with Teresa.

"She disappeared at the same time that he wished to lay hands on her to stop her. He travelled three whole months. She did not fail every day to show herself and bring his food. Finally he came to a cold green river which was very rapid and did not appear fordable; but there were some trees fallen across the breadth of the rapids. There was a piece of cleared land and he noticed at the entrance of the forest a little cabin. After he shouted repeatedly, a man finally came out and told him he is at the village of spirits and that all the souls are now assembled in his cabin where they are dancing in order to heal the Great Spirit's wife who is sick. 'But do not fear to enter. When you come in, take a gourd with which you can keep the soul of your sister.'"*

* The source of this legend is from *The Jesuit Relations* of 1636.

Brian's face looked glum as he listened by the firelight on the open Wyoming prairies.

" 'I am he who keeps the brains of the dead; when you have recovered the soul of your sister, return this way and I will give you her brain.' When he entered the cabin, the spirits were very frightened at the sight of this living man, and they vanished in an instant. At evening, very gradually they returned as he sat by the crackling log fire and they began to dance a great deal. As they danced, he made a great many attempts to bag his sister's soul into the gourd. The brave brother returns by way of his host, who gives him in another gourd the brain of his sister, and informs him of all he must do in order to get her back to life. 'Go to her grave,' says he, 'and carry her body to your cabin and make a feast. When all the guests are assembled take it on your shoulders and make a turn through the cabin holding two gourds in your hand. As soon as you have done this she will immediately come to life again. But *no* one must see what you have done.' Unfortunately a curious one raised his eyes, and his sister's soul escaped."

Brian imagined Iguk, Sam, and Peter gathered around his cabin to see Teresa revived, but one of them looked up, and she was gone.

At sunrise everyone was busy loading up horses with butchered meat and buffalo hides when Washakie shouted:

"Soldiers coming!"

All quickly mounted and rode toward the icy Wind River Mountains. But the soldiers slowly caught up and started firing. Brian turned around in his saddle, aimed with his rifle at a soldier carrying company colors and fired. He heard a scream and saw that he had winged a man with blond hair. Was it private Smith? He couldn't tell. Brian fired again and wounded an older grey-haired officer. Perhaps it was Shaughnessy, he didn't know.

"Good shooting," Washakie cried out.

But Brian kept on firing as if the Americans were British. Soon the troopers halted and gave up their chase. One of the soldiers eyed them through binoculars. After ten minutes of hard, steady riding, the Shoshones pulled into a damp hallow and rested.

"Brian, you do not despair of wounding your own kind?" Washakie asked.

"I'm Irish first, and white second, not the other way about."

"If you ever get back to Ayeland, those British will have to be on their guard."

Steven laughed aloud with his laughter ringing into the corners of the cowshed. *"You said it man. The Tommies will have to be on their guard. Me and Michael's goin' to even things up tomorrow, we are."*

That evening Brian didn't pay much attention to anything that was said at the pipe smoking ceremony. He wanted the ceremony to end so he and Chilsipee could crawl into their buffalo bed. By late evening, after a noisy chokecherry wardance, they finally had each other to themselves until mountain chickadees chirped early the next day which came with mist.

Brian opened his tepee flap where he smelled a strange aroma coming from outside. He saw eight men seated around a stretched buffalo hide steaming with hot water poured over its surface. After a few minutes they did the same with another large hide. They cut the seared hide into four pieces and put sand and a glue-like substance between two hides and "cooked" them into an object some four feet tall. Brian walked up to the men and gestured. They let him hold one of the finished products. It was tough as rock.

"Shield," one of them said in broken English. "Warrior shield."

"Aye, good work, shockin' good work!"

One of the men painted some red and yellow animal symbols in the dry outer surface for decoration or perhaps for explaining who the owner was as animals symbolized their ancient heritage. Brian reflected that a wolf or deer heritage was as important to the Indian as a feudal baronage to an Englishman like his own Earl of Chapwick.

"Brian, come my love, we go fish," shouted Chilsipee dressed in buckskins.

"Fish? Oh aye. I ain't fished since Lough Gowna!"

Chilsipee carried a large willow sprig funnel that looked like a squid.

"You catch fish with that?"

"Aye, me catch fish, love. You watch."

They approached a small stream with lots of deep pockets. Chilsipee placed the trap in one of the gurgling pockets and walked along the bank for a few minutes picking choke-cherries and gooseberries. Brian followed suit and ate more than he picked. For a moment he was back in Ireland with Teresa. They walked up to the willow trap, and his Indian wife gave it a yank. Three big rainbow trout squirmed and splashed in the icy waters.

"Now we have buffalo, trout and berries to eat tonight."

By the time they reached camp, it began to snow lightly. Bitter, sharp winds whirled the snow around the freezing pine-needled ground. It was good to get into the warmth of the tepee.

"Chilsipee, what are all those bundles hanging on sticks outside the warrior's tepees?"

"Medicine bundles, Brian. Each brave must have his medicine. It is woman's duty to guard it while her man hunts in the prairies or mountains."

"Aye. We have somethin' like that with our people in Ireland who give the cure. They have their medicine, too. Do you have any Medicine Men in this tribe, Chilsipee?"

"Yes, we have two. They give 'cure' as you say."

"How do they become Medicine Men?"

"Well, my uncle is one; his name in English White Hawk. You have met him at our council fires."

"Oh aye, I didn't know he was a Medicine Man."

Chilsipee giggled at his ignorance, for her uncle wore the colorful dress of a Medicine Man.

"Anyway, Brian, he told me what he had to do as young man."

The wind howled outside, and they could hear sleet and snow pelting the outside walls of the tepee.

"He had to test his bravery when he come to believe he be holy man. He must sleep by roaring waters of a place in English call Bull Lake where ghost of grey-white buffalo bull lives."

"Chilsipee, ya know, when I was comin' out here from Fort Laramie, I thought I seen a light grey buffalo bull out in the prairies."

"It means if you were Shoshone you be Medicine Man, Brian." She embraced him and moved her fingers through his hair. "You got much medicine, Brian, when you in that cave."

"Aye, but that was sad medicine."

"Well, Uncle White Hawk, he had to sleep by waters which roar with bellowing of grey bull. He did without being frightened, and they made him go into high mountains for vision."

"Ya know, Goo-choo-doah found me after I'd come from a bloody high mountain, over yonder."

"My uncle have vision of his soul going up into the sun, and they made him Medicine Man. You have vision up there too, Brian?"

"No, not like in the cave, but when the sun rose up over the prairies and my mountain's shadow spread west . . . Do you people worship the sun?"

"In summers we have sun dance, but it only a way of giving thanks to Great Spirit, not the sun."

"Oh aye. What is the dance like?"

"Men dance backward and forward blowing eagle-bone whistle. Skewers are stuck in their breasts with lines up to sacred cottonwood pole. If their flesh tear, they not pure. Very long dance. Two, three day when sun is brightest in sky."

"What do you believe about this Great Spirit. Is he God?"

"Yes. He order our lives and our mother earth. If we break his will by grabbing too much for self, he destroys little man."

"It's a bloody wonder he hasn't destroyed England!"

"Bloody wonder must wait. England—if she do what you say to Ayrland—will die someday. May take while."

Steven interjected out loud, *"Not if I have anything to do with it—it won't take too long."*

Michael groaned in his sleep beneath silvery Slieve Gullion. Mists began to form on its slopes.

One bright October day Brian asked Chilsipee to go for a walk with him into the mountains. They both wore heavy buffalo robes and plodded through occasional crusty drifts of snow. She pointed to a mountain called "Pa cup" (ice), and they walked toward it. Pert little grey Canada jays skipped from branch to branch begging for food. Chilsipee threw them a wee crumb she found in her beaded pouch. The squawking of these birds attracted smaller grey and black mountain chickadees. Brian and Chilsipee climbed higher through the woodlands up to timberline where pines grew squat, twisted and gnarled by the ever-howling winds.

"Rest, Brian?"

"Aye, let's sit over here by that tree trunk."

He put his arm around her and huddled close. They looked out over icy, barren uplands looking like the Steppes of Russia.

"Shall we climb higher, love?"

"Aye, if ya'd like. I had an old friend who thought trees were sacred," said Brian feeling the bark of the tree at their backs.

"Oh, we think so, too. Cottonwood tree down in valley very sacred!"

They edged around a stony knoll beyond the tree where they were and looked down on six bighorn sheep walking calmly some twenty feet below them.

"Look Brian, at our brothers with horns."

"Handsome folk enough they are!"

Storm clouds of grey and silver began to gather over the nearby peaks. The summit of "Pa cup" loomed above them only several hundred feet, but thick ice harassed them every inch of the way. After fifty feet or so, they came to the base of a hard packed snowfield that encrusted the crest of the mountain as far as they could see.

"You go up to top, love; I wait here for you. I been up there in summer—it lonely, lovely place."

"Aye, no, you come with me, Chilsipee. I want to share it with you."

They chopped steps in the snow with an old limber pine branch and worked their way up the white slope. Half way up, they stopped to rest and look at the windy, wild country. The wind robbed them of their breath as they began to inch their way to the summit. Brian elbowed his way over the last icy ridge and pulled up Chilsipee after him. They stood and stared into a hundred miles of space and kissed each other. The warmth of their hearts more than made up for the bitter cold.

"See tepee smoke way down yonder, love?"

"Aye. One of them is ours, and let's go back to it now. I could eat a whole buffalo."

"You have all you want, love, and I pour you lot of hot chokecherry sauce."

They trudged on down the slope of "Pa cup" to the forests and valleys below looking forward to their feast and their night together. After a superb meal of roasted buffalo laced with chokecherry sauce, Brian felt like learning a little of her language and asked, "Chilsipee, how do you say the days of the week starting with Sunday?"

"da vay mean day. So listen: Be ah da vay, Naw zee thup da vay, Wah naw da vay, Dees ah da vay, Te da way gay da vay, Goiee ye da vay and Mu da vay."

"Shoshone's as bad as Gaelic—I'll have a shockin' time learning it!"

Then they talked of the tribe's most famous woman, Sacajawea, whose name meant throw-the-boat and how she married a Frenchman and helped white father's men find passage to the West. Chilsipee thought she gave her tribe honor while her cousins did not. It was the likes of her cousins who forced Chief Washakie into having Brian thrown into a hunger cave. They talked of Irish heroes like Brian Boru and Wolfe Tone.

"When he talk, Brian, he talk in wolf's tone?"

Brian chuckled, "aye, maybe that's how he got his name. What a woman you are, Chilsipee!"

They talked into wee hours of the morning and fell asleep in each other's arms on a comfortable turkey feather mat.

Weeks flowed into months as Brian slowly learned what it is to be Shoshone. He could converse in Shoshone (with an Irish brogue) by midwinter. And by late winter Chilsipee was five months pregnant. All the snow and howling winds put him to mind of Ireland during the famine and then of Ireland before the famine. He pictured green rolling fields of his homeland which normally stayed green even in winter. He had the urge to write down his thoughts in the form of a poem and grabbed a burnt stick and wrote and rewrote the lines of a short poem on some soft dear hide. He called it "Irish November":

Strands of ivy, green and shiny
Cling to trees, void of leaves
Lining brey, misty and grey
Over fields green with a sheen
Of raindrops and pearls.

Not as wordy as Allingham, he thought, but at least he said his say, and his Indian woman liked it. She said she'd like to see his homeland someday.

By March the tribe's food supply had become dangerously low, and Chief Washakie rounded up men on snowshoes for a winter buffalo hunt. Brian waved goodbye to his wife and told her he'd be back in a week's time. Signs of spring were in the air. Aspen buds were popping and the winds were calmer. Deep snow drifts remained only in shaded areas. After one day's walk out in the prairie, Brian stood guard while his friends trudged right up to the flanks of some buffalo waddling through deep patches of snow. The arrows hit home, and he could hear the bulls scream in rage. Everything seemed to be going well.

But who was this coming up to Brian? He was riding faster in snow than anyone he had ever seen. Old White Hawk approached Brian with a solemn face while his pony snorted. The Medicine Man searched for words:

"My son, you must go. You must leave for your Ayeland."

"Why? I have to get Chilsipee first. Are the soldiers coming?"

"You must go without her, my son." Tears came to his eyes.

"No, I won't, she and I talked about goin' back to Ireland!"

By this time, other members of the hunting party approached Brian and White Hawk. Chief Washakie remained in deep silence.

"She dead, my son. Her belly slit open by soldiers. They kill many. I don't think they knew Chilsipee was yours,

111

but she was only woman in camp with child. It must have gotten back to Fort where you were. Come son, I will show you way to Grandmother's Land."

Brian fell to the ground and pounded and cursed the snow. He whimpered and cried and kicked over a scrawny tree.

"Go to hell old man. She's not dead anymore than I am."

"But you are dead, son. A piece of you just died."

"Oh God, my God."

White Hawk beckoned him to mount on his pony, and they rode off toward Montana, while Chief Washakie waved his hand mournfully and shouted.

"This is our battle, son. You have yours to fight back in Ayeland."

Brian just nodded with his reddened eyes and wild look. His mind was blank for the rest of the day. When they got to a high pass, White Hawk pointed the way to Canada fifteen sleeps to the north and gave him his fine pony. He had packed a few beaver pelts on the horse's side for Brian to sell along the way.

"Go my son, gain your freedom, and we will try to gain ours."

CHAPTER X

Return of a Native

With his beaver pelts and fine Indian pony sold, Brian walked the muddy streets of Seattle in early June, 1853. He had more than enough passage money to sail for Europe, and he had more than enough memories of Chilsipee to float through the sea of his mind. Gulls circling in foggy skies were a welcome relief from the dry and penetrating vastness of the Rocky Mountain West. He remembered mountain chains on end and his strange icy dreams of late April after he left his Shoshone people. Chilsipee spoke to him as a head on a pole, and so did his little sister Teresa. Surely Teresa wasn't a little girl of six or seven, but, for Brian she was frozen, as in death, at that age. Perhaps he held her spirit in a gourd. Chilsipee talked with Teresa and Flanigan and Brady and even his father and mother. They were all bound to or a part of the pole yet resisted not the merging of self with something larger. They could all talk simultaneously about different things, yet they all spoke about the same thing: what one man dreams all men do.

God it was cold up on those passes in Montana. Brian woke up once shivering cold. He could hear the blood squeak through his veins in the silence of the night. The moon even seemed to grind on its axis across the black sky. He went back to sleep after getting blood to circulate back in his feet and dreamed of a Shoshone campground on the shores of Walden Pond. Washakie came up to John Field and dragged him off to a hunger cave where his needs and wants would be equally simple. Then, as the blood-red sun rose, a harmless pine marten waddled past his head, and Brian screamed in terror thinking he was on the moon. Where else could one hear blood in his veins and see Wind River Mountains and Walden Pond at the same time? Grey clouds sailed at him from the mountain tops like Chilsipee's outstretched arms, and swirls of dust whirled around and around from the valleys below like troopers pursuing Indians or British land-lords pursuing tenants or . . . for a moment he thought he was going insane, incredibly insane. Why couldn't he just explode into parts and settle down as dust engrained into lichens and liverworts.

Those green and windy plains of Alberta waved and thumped in his brain. God, the way the wind cracked those prairie grasses flowing up to the incredibly icy, grey striated Rocky Mountains. No U.S. trooper could ensnare him up here in Canada! Was it far to Dorine's and Grosse Isle? It must be. One more pass, one more ice field and I'll be in Pacific Canada. God, I can almost smell the salt air! Grizzly bears have nothing on me for my very mind is as grizzly as a crusty old lichen or liverwort.

Brian's mind floated up and out of his body and sifted down to his Irish farm where he drank steaming hot tea and thought of North America. God it's good to be back in Ireland. Look at those greenbreys, but . . . I'm still in Amer-ica, or is it Canada? Who can say where man's mind is? Is Seattle part of British Canada or America? It depends on when you ask. Perhaps Quebec will someday be part of France or who knows what. Isn't it silly to think that Brian was walking in a lumber town called Seattle when he was really fishing with Chilsipee? How could anyone be foolish enough to think he really is in North Square or Fort Laramie? No, no, no man is where he's supposed to be. He's a thousand places at once. Just because your rear end is bouncing up and down on horseback in Wind River Canyon doesn't mean your brains are. This Brian McBride—who in God's name is he? Oh, those damn Montana hills. Those lonely Alberta prairies and icefields. Gulls screamed with laughter, and Brian found himself in Seattle. Seattle where?

114

"Where in Ireland, are ya from, me good man?"

"County Cavan."

"It couldn't be, is it? Brian, Brian McBride wearin' Indian clothes," a stranger said as he approached closer.

"Why, yes. I'm Brian, but . . . who the devil are you . . . ?"

"Davis Ryan! Don't ya remember me? From the *Pinzance*. I thought I recognized you from behind that beard hummin' an Irish tune and talking to yerself in an Irish brogue."

"Davis . . . are you the bloke . . . that lost a babe at sea?"

"Aye. But ya don't have to go remindin' me of that now, do ya?"

"Sorry. I've lost a good share, too. But what brings ya to these parts—all the way from Grosse Isle?"

"Me woife and I settled in the prairies of western Canada. But I lost her to the cholera a year ago yesterday. We had a farm at the foot of the Rockies and grew wheat, lots of wheat. I came out here hopin' to find work as I couldn't bear those lonely Canadian winds without Cathy. And yerself—what brings *you* here?"

Brian told him of his Shoshone days and Chilsipee. He didn't have much good to say about the U.S. government but expressed his admiration for certain Americans like the Negro and Chief Washakie.

"My God, Brian. It sounds like you need religion, man. Ya need to get to some comfort right quick. If I hadn't my faith, I'd a killed myself after seein' Cathy die. I had lots of wheat, but what's wheat without love. Let's you and me go to a wee gatherin' of Catholics down by the waterfront. It's the Sabbath, ya know."

"Catholic? I'm Protestant, Davis, a bloody Protestant."

"Ah forget yer Old World prejudices and come to mass with me. The priest there is a shockin' philosopher he is. I'm just on my way to mass. It's the Sabbath ya know. Our mass is held out in open for want of a chapel."

"Sure I'm not dressed for the occasion."

"Pay no mind to how yer dressed and come with me Brian. Ya have to listen to this man."

"But I don't understand Latin—it may as well be Chinese."

"And you after learnin' Shoshone! Anyway, his sermon will be in English, Brian."

He went to please his fellow countryman more than anything else. They walked a few rods toward the primitive wharves and entered a small crowd gathered in a circle. The priest was dressed in long dark robes and opened with the first part of the Latin mass, the Order of the mass. The flickering candles, incense, and crucifix fascinated Brian. Somehow he was reminded of Shoshone ceremonial rituals. Was the priest incensing the four cardinal directions?

This sandy-haired priest left the make-shift altar to enter the midst of the gathering and preached a sermon he would never forget:

"Who was this Jesus? What was he like? What were his thoughts? Sure, we've all seen sweet pictures of Jesus in Aunt Bessie's living room back home. But who was he? You know, he was a kind of rebel in his day. What he preached would be considered scandalous today. Take for instance the parable of the Good Samaritan. To put it in modern terms, a European immigrant lay injured in the Oregon woods, and he asked for help. An American settler passed him by. Then a British landholder refused to give him aid. Who helped him but a Nez Perce Indian! If Christ were alive today, we'd crucify him all over again because he would upset our social stability." Brian eyed the crucifix behind the priest.

"Yes, Jesus would cast a stern glance on those who make endless profits from the poor: on those who rob the Indians of their rightful lands: on those who are smug in their own self-satisfaction: on those who have caused others' suffering. His Sermon on the Mount, if it were preached today in the financial centers of London or New York, what do you think bankers and brokers would say? 'Blessed are the poor, for theirs is the Kingdom of Heaven?' No, they would pronounce Christ as a radical revolutionary. For too long now

Christians have called themselves Christians without knowing who Christ was, who He is. As you eat His Body and drink His Blood this morning in this village of Seattle, reflect upon His words and His actions. Amen!"

Steven started singing a catchy version of "Amen" he had heard at mass in Dublin a few months back: *"Yes Amen, yes Amen, yes Amen, Amen. Oh yes Amen, yes Amen, yes Amen, Amen, Amen."* Michael asked what time it was and when he heard it was only 3:30 a.m., he rolled back in the hay for more sleep. Only a suggestion of pink tinged Slieve Gullion.

Davis and Brian left the crowd and entered a world of sea gulls laughing on top of wooden framed buildings: of ships plying through green waters: of bearded beggars on the sidewalks: of flags flying in the breeze. But what on earth was that tall pole with heads carved on it? My God, it looks like Wolfe Tone and all, Brian thought to himself. One of the figures looked like it was holding a gourd.

"Davis, am I seein' things? What is that pole?"

"Sure its only a totem pole the Indians made."

"Totem pole?"

"Yes, a pole of an Indian clan which all members are related in the same way, say to a bear or elk, at least that's what they told me when I asked after I saw them for the first time."

"Can all the people on the pole speak at the same time?"

"I s'pose if they could speak, yes, but it's only carved wood."

"Aye, aye. I think I understand. What one man dreams other men do."

"Yer not clear, but I guess I catch yer meanin'. Anyway, Brian are ya goin' back to the old country or what?"

"Aye, indeed I am. It's not that I don't love this wild, wild land, but somethin' inside me is pullin' me back. I'da stayed, if Chilsipee was alive. I've got a wee sister back in Dublin I must tend to."

"Ya know, if I had the money, I'd go with ya. All I'm doin' is sort of flounderin' around Seattle without any . . . I don't know purpose I s'pose. I'da stay, too, if Cathy had, lived."

"Well Davis, yer in luck. I have over fifteen pounds sterling in me pockets from sellin' beaver pelts and a pony at a Canadian fur trading post. And if necessary, why couldn't we work aboard a ship that's goin' back?"

"Aye. Yer right, man yer right! There's a good many timber ships in port. I don't know if any's goin' ta Ireland or not."

They wandered about the wharves and soon discovered that several ships were loading up with wood to set sail for Glasgow or Plymouth. They checked into one called *Columbia* and were told if they paid five pounds each and worked for their keep, the two of them could have passage in just eight days. She was to sail around the Horn and north to Scotland.

Davis and Brian walked over to a sawmill and managed to get employment while they waited for their ship to sail. They learned, over the days, how the Americans claimed this territory just a few years back when British union jacks flew so proudly. The British were pushed north of the forty-ninth parallel.

"Ya know," Brian said to one of the American lumber-men, "if we Irish had any wits, we'd get rid of the union jacks flyin' over Irish skies."

"Why don't ya," asked a burly blond-haired fellow.

"We will, indeed. But ya know it takes more than changin' a flag ta get rid of the British. Ya got ta declare cultural independence. Look at yous here in America. Yer still British in dress, manner, and language, and ya kill off those who have strange religions and who wear feathers in their hair."

"What would you have us do—go to Seattle with feathers in our hair?"

"Indeed I would! Why don't yous intermarry and learn some of the Indian ways and language?"

"It's easy to talk about somethin', Irishman, when ya ain't done it yourself."

Davis interrupted, "Indeed he has!"

"Well," snapped the American, "That's just plum crazy—that's all. Someday the whole world will be like America, yes sir. Even the far off jungles of Asia, yep. Why when people that's savages sees what we got, they won't want anythin' diffrint."

"Don't you see," Brian retorted, "that yer still British in yer outlook! What yer sayin' is what the British have said to the Irish and to yous before the Revolution."

Brian got punched in the eye and tumbled over sideways into a saw blade that tore open his stomach. The pain paralized him like a thousand needles of ice.

"Tell him I didn't mean ta hurt him that bad," the American lumberman said.

Brian passed out when he saw blood and some intestine oozing out from his wound. He was back in Drogheda with Sam Brady, though he never knew Sam until he got to Massachusetts. Coal smoke permeated the air with stinging acidity. They walked up a steep, hilly street lined with grey pebbledashed buildings containing bed and breakfast hotels, butcher shops, and bakeries. Blood sausage hung in strings behind steamed up windows. They caught the scent of freshly killed chicken and pigs. They ambled past the bakery with newly baked wheaten bread and juicy peach tarts. Ahead of them lay McDaniel's pub emitting the aroma of sawdust and stale beer.

"What say we have a wee nip, Brian? Look's like it's gona start rainin' somethin' fierce, anyway."

"Aye, I'm feelin' a strong thirst."

They entered the dark pub where a man with a flute played Irish airs in the back of the room. Sam ordered two porters and paid with an American dollar. The brew tasted bitter and strong like stale and moldy chokecherry sauce. It rained hard while they chatted and ordered two more pint glasses. Then a strong sun beamed down on the rain-soaked streets.

"There's a shockin' foine hill out of town called Mulley's Brey, Brian. Would ya like to take a wee ramble up it?"

"Aye, indeed."

Grey old Drogheda nestled along the shores of the silvery River Boyne faded behind them as they crossed damp green fields of uncut oats and entered a thick woodland of oaks, hemlock and larch. They barely made out the ruins of some prehistoric mound deep in the dark woods where the sun did no good. Finally, they emerged by a wee lake and started climbing up a slope of pink-flowered heather and prickly whin bushes. Patches of stinging nettle grew in and around blackberry vines laden with juicy berries. Mulley's Brey's velvety summit rose high above, seemingly distant and un-approachable. They paused to rest a moment to be startled by the sudden fluttering of a white willy wagtail flying for safety from human intruders. In the far valleys below, several magpies, citizens of both continents, hovered in the air . . . Brian moaned a little . . . the slopes of Mulley's Brey, or was it "Pa cup"? looked white. Sam looked like . . . Chilsipee.

"Chilsipee. You're not dead!"

"White Hawk forced to tell you I am dead. Haters of Sacajawea want to get rid of you, love. If I leave with you . . . they kill us both." Brian screamed aloud in his sleep back at Seattle. Chilsipee had Sam Brady's face now, and they climbed higher. They could hear wind in the Wyoming Irish pines and farmers' voices. Everything seemed so calm and peaceful. Then sudden bursts of rifle fire rang out in the green and rainy valleys below. Sam and Brian descended a small vale into a thick and oozing peat bog with clumps of ferns and rich green moss. Part of the bog had been cut to drain. A few prehistoric toothless bogmen stood by their

shovels waving hello as black crows and choughs flew over-
head. They had to be careful crossing the bog as one false
step could mean they'd be up to their hips in oozing peat.
They got across and climbed up some steep granite rocks
covered with loose and treacherous moss. Sam slipped and
grabbed an exposed root to fall over backwards thirty feet
down into a small dead oak tree which came crashing down
on Sam.

"Go on, son, you can . . . easily . . . climb . . . to the
summit . . . I'm done for."

Brian climbed higher and ate some chokecherries, or was it
blueberries to look across a grand and glistening bay to a
high mountain in the North called Slieve Gullion. No, surely
Chilsipee's uncle, a medicine man, wouldn't lie. No, he
wouldn't lie. He climbed to the top of Mulley's Brey among
huge piles of stone that the legendary Irish giant Finn
MacCool must have put up there.

When he woke up, he found himself on a cot in some
small cabin with a pile of bandages on his stomach. A little
old man wearing spectacles told him he just put thirty
stitches in and that his stomach would smart a while.

"But how will I get to me homeland?"

"Nothin' preventin' ya from gettin' aboard a ship in five
or six days. You won't be able to work much . . . but yer
alive, ain't ya? Ya owe me twenty dollars, man."

"Twenty dollars equals what in pounds?"

"I'll settle for five pounds," which he took.

Davis managed to find that sandy-haired priest who had
some words of comfort for Brian:

"When you're back in Ireland, all this will be nothing
more than a dream, son, just a dream."

"Aye, but dreams are as real as life, aren't they?"

"Yes, perhaps so. We must have our dreams, son, we
must. Without dreams hope for Christian unity in all parts
of the western world is sheer folly."

"Aye, and for personal unity, too."

They had been at sea for twenty days before Brian could give a hand with the rigging helping hoist sails and swab down the deck while the California coast inched past. Some evening brought pain to him that he thought he couldn't endure. But there were other kinds of pain. Davis and Brian were the only two Irishmen aboard a Scottish ship. Brian, however, was treated with more courtesy because of his religion. No matter how many times Brian reminded the sailors of the parable of the Good Samaritan, he heard back in Seattle, they just chuckled and jeered.

"Mics ain't worth beina gud Samare-tan furr," one of them would say. Man is cursed with ignorance, Brian thought to himself. As the *Columbia* sailed past the palm studded Mexican coast, Brian wondered how they could possibly be going to Europe. The earth was becoming stranger and stranger. It shouldn't look like this—all those black lava rocks and lime-green seas. Would they ever get back to Ireland, or would only his mind make the journey.

They put into a small Colombian seaport for supplies in pale blue seas. Dark, pine-clad foothills fingered their way down to the shoreline from misty Incan heights above. As the last barrels of salted fish were being loaded on board, a strange, almost supernatural rumbling was heard. The wooden beams of wharves and docks groaned like a dying old man. Dust sifted from adobe buildings along the shore. A large cactus plant split in half, and the previously calm ocean waters thrashed like a thousand sharks madly pursuing some drowning man. The captain ordered the ship to put out to sea immediately to get away from the devastation of a Columbian earthquake. God what a strange land! The only time the earth rumbles in Ireland is when the head of Scotland crunches that frightened Irish puppy dog.

Davis was spat upon somewhere off the coast of Chile. Poor old Davis turned in early that starry night to think alone in his wee bunk and listen to the splashing wake of the ship. Three of the crew members burst in upon him with a crucified chicken cackling for life. They nailed it to the wall.

"Now ya can pray, mick! We made a Catholic alter fer ya!"

Davis shivered in rage thinking of the *Pinzance* and Cathy and Kevin. Why, in God's name did they ever leave Ireland for the far prairies of Alberta? The Scottish crewmen roared with laughter.

"Looks like da mick squire's gon looney, eh what?"

Brian came tramping into the cabin after mending some canvas sails and shouted at the Scottsmen to get the hell out. Davis was on the verge of a nervous breakdown except for Brian's comfort and companionship. The Catholic Irishman's hair grew greyer by the weeks. Ireland, oh Ireland! Oh God, those treacherous Straits of Magellan with icebergs and grey sleet.

Now Brian had some idea of Iguk's land at the opposite pole. All this ice and snow. How could anyone say "Aja, it is good?" The whole ship suddenly disappeared in a "white out" where everything became astoundingly white and fuzzy. Then strange electric cracklings resounded through the air. Only very slowly did the ship's rigging appear along with white crusty ice floating in grey waters. Is Baffinland like this? What strange little penguins waddling along the frozen shoreline! They looked like miniature troopers back at Fort Laramie. He was glad he no longer had to take orders from an unthinking penguin like Shaughnessy. Perhaps these Straits are the tunnel you have to go through to reach the after life whited out from life itself. Brian momentarily wandered back to the Saint Lawrence River and the Isle of Anticosti. Canadian and Argentine shorelines interlaced. Opposite poles fused and crackled. British soldiers chased Indians and American cavalrymen charged through the bogs of Ireland. Is my own soul in a gourd? Who has the gourd? Ireland, get us back to Ireland! Those lonely naked shores of Tristan de Cunha. Give us some Allingham, oh Lord. Off the Canary Islands, Brian woke up feeling the lump scar on his belly and screaming for Chilsipee. I wonder if she could tell me her inmost thoughts since she had to speak in English for me? My poor, dead Chilsipee. This voyage would test the patience of Job, and then some. Creaking timbers, Scottish brogue, ocean, ocean, and more ocean. What the hell kind of planet is this? His friend Davis was nearly mad with rage over months of insults. But it would be better for him when he returned to live with his uncle. Brian resorted to fantasizing about being back in his homeland until he saw the river Clyde and Glasgow harbor echoing with the laughter of gulls. After a night's stay in a dingy little waterfront inn, Davis seemed better. Nothing like solid land! Both men embarked for Ireland aboard a cattle boat the next evening sailing across the Irish Sea. They parted ways forever in the port of Belfast.

"Sure I'll be fine now, once I get to me uncle's. Go find that wee sister of yers," Davis said as he waved goodbye.

CHAPTER XI

Back to Slieve Gullion

Sipping a cup of strong tea, Brian sat on an old wooden chair waiting for his sister to come to his two room farm house beneath the Mountains of Mourne in County Down. October winds had tinged the misty hedgerows with a touch of cranberry-red. Swaying ash trees rustled in damp breezes combing through their green leaves just fringed with pale yellow. Grey clouds built up over the emerald green summit of Slieve Gullion. He had been back in Ireland some two months now and, after much difficulty, located Teresa in a Dublin brewery where she worked. Elish, his cousin, was still working at the mill in Rathmines and told Brian, whom she didn't recognize at all, where his sister could be found. When Brian showed up at this dingy brewery six and a half years later, Teresa refused to accept that Brian was really Brian:

"I'm sorry, sir, as much as I'd like to believe ya, I know me brother's dead, for I ain't heard from him since he left Ireland back in ... 1847 ... and me gory if it ain't 1854 now ... surely a brother would take the trouble of sendin' word to his sister if he were alive. Besides he didn't have no beard and wasn't as dark complected as you are." Deep inside, this beautiful black-haired thirteen year old girl knew it was her brother, but she wanted to play the martyr after so long without any close kin.

"Teresa, I wrote you care of Elish probably twenty times. Somehow me letters didn't get through to ya. Whether she held them up for her own reasons, I don't know. Yer lookin' shockin' fine ... " He noticed her indifference and said in an annoyed tone, "Ah, stop playin' games wid me. Ya know damn well I'm yer brother. We lived in a ditch together, buried our father, and went through the soup kitchens of Dublin."

Teresa broke down and wept. She realized her cruelty had gone too far:

"But Brian, how in Lord's name ... I mean why for God's sake ... haven't you ... I mean ... " and she cried steadily almost in hysteria. Brian comforted her and began with his long story of his stay in North America:

"But why didn't you take another Indian wife, Brian?"

"I could think of no one but Chilsipee."

"But why didn't you try to go back to Fort Laramie?"

"You can't go back to somethin' ya don't believe in, Teresa."

"But why didn't you stay in Seattle?"

"What, after I had me belly ripped open?"

"But why didn't ya go back to Boston?"

"I knew if I must do anything, it must be here in Ireland. Sure, America had claimed its independence from the British, but I knew we must claim complete cultural independence here in Ireland. We must go back to our Gaelic language and to our own ways and customs! Those poor people in America can never break ties with England because English is their language. It isn't likely they'll switch to Shoshone or Sioux or some combination of Indian tongues. But we Irish have a long history, just like the Shoshone, and we have a whole bloody island to turn back into Ireland, not West Briton! We have something to go back to, while Americans, unless they stop killing their only native link to North America, have nothing to go back to. That's why it will take centuries for them to find themselves. Maybe the land will claim them and turn them into North Americans. But we Irish already are Irish, for God's sake, let's *stay* Irish!"

"Brian, yer a changed man since I seen ya last. God, I don't even understand what yer sayin', but I know you believe what yer sayin'."

"Teresa, I'm gona have to find us a farm to rent somewhere, and when I find one, I'll send word to Elish. Now you take care, little one, and we'll see each other soon."

"Brian, I meant ta give ya this." She handed him a bottle of dark porter which he opened and drank slowly and steadily. As he wiped his lips, he said in a low tone of voice, "God that was good."

"Brian, I have over ten pound saved . . . if that will help us . . . I was savin' ta go look for ya in America . . . but . . . "

"Grand, Teresa, grand. Ten pound will get us potato seed next spring, and I have enough for to buy some food and turf, if necessary."

"Wait just a minute, Brian. What ever became of that school teacher ya went on the boat with?"

"The poor man died of typhus. But t'was in Canada he died. Happy enough he was to have seen the wild continent and a native Eskimo."

"What in land's name is an Eskimo?"

"A foine copper-colored chap who lives off the land where ice stays year round."

"Me gory if we don't have a bit of catchin' up ta do with all you've been through."

"Aye, and I suppose you've been through—a good bit yourself."

"Nothin' like you. I best be gettin' back to work now, or they'll be callin' fer me."

"Aye. I'll send fer ya once I find a place to stay."

Brian went north to County Cavan and found no trace of the Harriscs, Reverend Samuel or Gary. Their old homestead was just a shell of stone walls covered with ivy nettles and weeds. He couldn't find any grave markings of his parents amongst the patches of bright green shamrocks. Those hills of his childhood hounded him. He was miserable there in Cavan. Too many painful memories scratched his soul. So Brian headed northeast into County Down and found a wee farm for rent beneath the verdant slopes of Slieve Gullion. His landlord was a cantankerous old Scotch-Irish Presbyterian.

By the time Brian had finished his cup of strong tea, Teresa and Elish walked up the lane from Fork Hill into his front yard:

"It's grand, Brian, grand, I love it! We'll do alright here, we will."

"Aye, Brian, you and yer sister will fair well here. I best be going as I have a long journey back to Dublin."

"Ah sure, Elish, you'll stay for a boiled egg and tea!"

"No, I must be goin'. This is no time for me to be stayin'. Yous have too much to talk about without me interferin'." She felt guilty in having held back Brian's letters, but she felt they would torment Teresa more than help her. Elish left, and Brian just stared at Teresa in laughter and tears.

"So how are ya, wee sister?"

She giggled nervously and remarked,

"I see ya shaved off yer beard."

"Aye. I'm not on the American frontier no more. Sister, tomorrow I'm goin' down to Belfast for to buy some books. I've a lot of readin' to catch up on. I have to get a greater understandin' of me own native land as I farm this rich soil."

"So ya can read deep books, can you? As you wish, Brian. I shall tidy up the place and get in some more turf for the loft and see if I can buy us a hundred weight of spuds down at Fork Hill."

Brian waved goodbye to his sister and tramped north to the town of Newry where he would catch a train for Belfast. He passed rows of lush apple trees forming fruitful woods at the northern base of Slieve Gullion. God it was good to be back in the homeland smelling the damp earth, seeing willy wagtails flying about, hearing the cackle of choughs and

128

crows, watching curls of peat smoke rise from thatched cottages, seeing whinbush rustle in soft breezes, tasting tart blackberries from thick hedgerows, listening to the churning of a country stream over mossy rocks, and hearing Teresa's voice once again.

He looked up into the Mountains of Mourne and thought of Chilsipee and her gentleness and warmth. That crazy old willow fish trap of hers was a marvel indeed, and the way she said "love" made his soul crack. Then he thought of the Negro cook and prayed for his liberation. Maybe I should have taken him with me. Catholics call us black Irish—what would they call him? Brian passed a pile of rocks that reminded him of his hunger cave. But now he was in Ireland at long last, tramping the streets of Newry with its homes of grey stone and sooty chimneys.

After paying for his ticket, he hopped on the train powered by a steam locomotive and watched the Irish countryside whizz past him at thirty-five miles per hour. As the whistle screamed through the valleys, cows and goats stood in fields that raced by him as though they were on conveyor belts he had seen in mills. Hedgerows mixed with fields and lakes and hills so brilliant green blurred together until the train rolled into the yards of Belfast, the city where he had last seen Davis. He asked the stationmaster where he could go see books and was told to go to Queens College which had an enormous library.

"Sir, I'm afraid you cannot enter our library until you fill out a form," said a skinny young female clerk with bad breath.

"Aye, well then give me the form!"

He read it over and was amazed to see that they wanted to know how much schooling he had, who his major professor was, and what type of research he was doing, and why he wanted to use this particular library.

"Schooling," he asked aloud. "I'll put down Pa cup College with my major professor being—let's see, Major Professor Washakie. For research—oh, hell. Lady do ya want a bloody fist in yer face?"

"Shhhh!" hissed the bad breathed clerk.

"Just let me go in ta look around."

"Do you know how to use our catalog of books?"

"No. Show me!"

"I cannot as I must maintain my post."

Brian pushed right past her despite her protests, holding his nose and walking into the stack area to stare at thousands of books in rows on end of wooden shelves. He scratched his head and drifted about endlessly looking at titles that were of no interest to him whatsoever. After several hours he went up to a shelf at random and pulled off a book called Wolfe Tone's *Autobiography*. He sat down in a corner and read and read until sundown when he was told he would have to leave. What fascinated him most was the idea of a workers' unification of Protestants and Catholics to form a new government. Irish are Irish first, workers second, and members of religious bodies last.

"If only I could talk with me father now," Brian mumbled as he left the building. He slowly ambled down Royal Street past numerous bookstalls on side streets under cumbersome stone buildings reddening in the sunset.

By the end of the week, Brian had purchased over forty books, among them a beat up copy of Wolfe Tone's *Autobiography*, the King James' verson of the Bible, and various histories of Ireland. He thoroughly enjoyed chatting with the shopkeepers about books and about his life in America. He went to his first play, "She Stoops to Conquer," and his mind exploded with thoughts. When Brian returned to his farm, all he could do was talk about *ideas*, something so different for his sister who was accustomed to talk about *things* over the past six years.

"Brian, nobody talked of ideas in that dim old brewry in Dublin. We just washed bottles and pasted on labels and talked of lovely clothes that could be bought if ya had the money."

"Did ya stay with Elish all the while?"

"Aye, but except for Sunday afternoons when we'd go to Phoenix Park for a wee ramble, me life was dull. Sometimes we'd walk the banks of the River Liffey, but Elish didn't talk too much, especially when I brung up the matter of me brother."

"Well, we're here together now. Surely nothing will part us but death itself."

"Aye."

For months on end Brian did light farming and heavy reading. By the 1860's he had a collection of several scores of books, including the poems of William Allingham, Jonathon Swift's *Gulliver's Travels,* and various political writings. Brian met with numerous farmers and townspeople and talked of an Ireland free of British rule. However, none were willing to commit themselves to anything because they had been able to forget those years of famine.

One rainy November day, Brian had called several farmers together in an abandoned round tower not far away. It was a tall structure of crumbling stone covered with strands of ivy on a high brey overlooking distant Milltown Lake. A grove of pines hissed with each gust of rain and wind. Brian and a group of seven other farmers gathered in the musty old tower under gloomy skies.

"Me good old friend Peter Flanigan once told me that Ireland is the wrong Island. If only we could have been the closest one to the European continent, we would have gotten more help from the French in the days of Wolfe Tone," Brian stated cooly. His voice echoed faintly back and forth high in the tower.

"Ah, sure don't even talk to me of Wolfe Tone," one of the farmers burst out. "That bloke wanted Protestants and Catholics to unite as workers!"

"Aye," another farmer shouted. "And we know that's just not possible. Why just the other day in Crossmaglen we was walkin' home from church when a brave lot of Catholic women fresh out of mass wearin' their shawls spat on us tellin' us we were no damn good heathens. Imagine callin' *us* heathens."

"Aye, but we are Irish first," Brian shouted back. "What the hell did Britain do fer us durin' the famine, now? She gave us stale old Indian corn, that's what!"

"Brian, them days is over and 'tis best to forget them," a wee whisp of a man said sitting in some hay by the damp wall. "We can't go on carryin' grudges forever, now, can we? We have a great deal in common with the English, after all."

"Aye, because we were forced to—just like the Shoshone Indian peoples are bein' forced to live in smaller and smaller areas and eventually to speak English."

"But we ain't Indians—we is civilized," an angry farmer retorted. "Besides, them Indians, I hear tell, fight among themselves—so why can't we fight among ourselves?"

"You just called us civilized. How can we be civilized as long as we don't have our own land which was taken from us in the first place," Brian remarked. "What we need is to strike against the landlords and claim our own land!"

"If ya do that, Brian, you'll have ta do it yerself. We ain't in agreement," one of the group said. All their voices continued to echo.

Brian felt sick at heart. He turned his back on all those Protestants in that Catholic round tower and went out in the driving rains. He tramped the roads toward Newry for an hour or so passing a slovenly, dark-haired, shifty eyed country wench who made a vulgar gesture. Turning around, he grabbed her from behind and threw her into a ditch. When she raised her skirt, he couldn't resist her and climbed down into the mud and had her while hawthorn branches creaked in the rain soaked breezes. All the while she laughed aloud like an old crow. After he left her and climbed up into the misty breys above, he felt stupid and bad, even repulsed by his own asininity. "Never, never again," he mumbled to himself as he climbed the rising fields getting away from all people.

"God damned stupid fools people are, myself included," he shouted at the top of his lungs.

He climbed higher into a rocky area at the base of Slieve Gullion and picked up a sharp stone and carved a crude petroglyph in one of the rocks looking something like that figure back at the hunger cave. As the sun set, Brian recalled dimly lit tepees in drifted nighttime snow and the voice of his Chilsipee. He climbed higher up the slope to see the remains of a chambered cairn looking like a tepee ring or medicine wheel back in the American West. Just above this prehistoric ruins he saw to his surprise spiral patterns carved by ancient Celts on round rocks. He sat down under clearing skies and sensed a presence of something even stronger than he felt in those valleys of Wyoming. His primitive roots were as ancient as those of any Indian tribe.

"Here is our heritage. Let no union jack fly here to disturb our sense of who we are," Brian screamed aloud.

He knew something good would come of his feelings. Somehow they would prevail whether or not farmers in the valleys below were content with the status quo. Brian didn't know when or how he could do anything, but he knew he *would* despite the fact that his friends were few. He looked forward to getting back to his farm and sister. He could cultivate his fields for now, anyway.

The only person who really sympathized with him through the seasons was Teresa who gradually had learned how to read. Unfortunately by the time she was twenty-three, she developed a lung disease, probably inherited, which forced her to become a semi-invalid. Only on rare occasions did she struggle to get up and walk about. But it was she who convinced Brian to write down his life story in the form of a diary. She prodded him with questions about Fort Laramie or Iguk, enabling him to jot down details which he would have otherwise forgotten. While her health never really deteriorated, she seemed only to hold her own as a weak invalid. She was paying the price for her years in a damp brewery.

"Teresa, did ya hear tell of the Civil War over in America? I just read about it in the newspaper. Maybe my Negro friend back at Fort Laramie will gain his freedom yet."

"I hope so, Brian, it's shockin to think a man would be whipped for the color of his skin."

"Aye, but over here we're bein' whipped for the color of our thoughts. What we need to do is stir up these complacent farmers and workers with a new sense of what Ireland really is. If they lowered the union jack in Seattle, why can't we do the same in Newry, Belfast, and Dublin?"

"Now yer talkin' Brian. Now yer talkin'. Too damn bad ya can't step out of that diary and join me, man," Stephen said aloud one hundred and ten years later.

"Brian, I hope your dreams come to pass," Teresa said mournfully in the valleys of the Mountains of Mourne.

By the 1870's, Brian had to dream his dreams for a free Ireland alone with Teresa until the rise of a man called Charles Stewart Parnell.

CHAPTER XII

Ireland Forever!

As the sun rose and lit up the upper grasslands of Slieve Gullion, Steven, having finished the diary, sang out loud an IRA rebel song to awaken his partner, Michael:

> *In Ireland's fight for freedom, boys.*
> *The North has played her part,*
> *And though her day is yet to come,*
> *We never yet must part.*
> *We'll keep the fight until the end;*
> *We know we cannot fail.*
> *And there's the reason why today*
> *They keep our lads in Dublin jail.*
> *So join the fight you volunteers.*
> *It cannot be denied*
> *Until they break our spirits down,*
> *They just as soon have died.*
> *For England knows and England hates*
> *Our fearless northern men.*
> *And that's another reason why*
> *They keep our lads in Dublin jail!*

Michael woke up screaming, *"He made the sign of the cross backwards!"*

"What are ya talkin' about, Michael?"

*"The bloke that came to see us last night! Remember when he answered our question how do we know whether he is a British informer 'An old feeble Catholic man like me?' Well, he made the sign of the cross **backwards**, I tell ya!"*

"I'll run out and check to see if any tommies is comin'," snapped Steven.

He went out into the early morning mist and saw or heard no one and came back in. A lonely willy wag-tail fluttered off from a monkey puzzle tree.

"Sure ya were moanin' in yer sleep all last night. 'Twas only a dream ya had about the sign of the cross."

*"No, I tell ya, I seen it. That's what **made** me moan!"*

"Perhaps we should get movin', Michael, anyway."

"Aye, but let's have a wee spot of breakfast first."

"Aye."

They ate some rations and talked about joining up with their friends down in the valley at the chambered cairn, a favorite rendezvous point for modern rebels and ancient Druids. Steven told Michael about Brian up to the point of his return to Ireland and the rise of Parnell when out of nowhere fifteen British soldiers with their officer came racing into the grassy yard before the cowshed. Michael reacted quickly and hid their weapons in a deep hole which he covered with dung and hay.

"Okay, maites, up wid yer hands!" a tommy shouted.

"Right y'are sport," Steven snapped.

Another soldier wearing a camouflaged poncho hit Michael in the rump with the butt of his rifle:

"You, squire, where's yar guns?"

"We ain't got none. We dropped 'em in a ditch down at Fork Hill."

"We know yar lyin', squire! Where are they?"

"Search around if ya believe we have any!"

Five of the grim faced soldiers searched the cowshed stepping in the dung which covered their rifles.

"They musta hid 'em down below somewhere. Okay squires, up ya git. We're all goin' back ta Fork Hill fur questionin', so git movin'."

Michael asked Steven, *"What happened to Brian?"*

"Brian?" a British soldier asked. *"So there's one more of yous, eh?"*

"Aye," Steven said. *"Brian McBride. He's a Protestant like you, but he's for a free Ireland!"*

One of the tommies hit Steven in the jaw with a rifle butt, and blood oozed out of Steven's mouth. A distinguished looking British officer with a whisp of a moustache winced at his soldier's roughness.

"Ah sure Brian's only a dead man whose diary we bin readin'," Michael said to save his comrade.

"Ya know yer funny squire, very funny. We'll get ya a showin' at the Palladium in London, we will!" one tommy said to Steven. *"Move on you son of a bitch IRA trash!"*

"Easy on the language," the thoughtful, almost professorial officer shouted.

"I ain't no Shoshone," Steven played along, *"but maybe I am. This land is ours. We must be allowed to hunt our game. IRA and AIM must merge!"*

"We got ourselves a crazy here, maites! Shut yer gob you bastard IRA!"

"Easy on the language," commanded the officer.

"It's easy for you imperialists to tell us to shut up when . . . "

They knocked out Steven and dragged him along the ground until he came to.

"Now walk, you idiot!"

"Michael, let me tell ya what happened to Brian and how he met Parnell down in Cork," Steven panted.

"Aye. Yous tommies don't object to hearin' a story of a dead man do yous?"

"If it amuses you, Irishman, I should think it might prove interesting," remarked the officer.

Well Brian had become obsessed with the idea of Irish

independence and was disheartened by a Fenian rebellion being crushed in 1867. *Irish People*, their newspaper, came with regularity to the McBride farm. He joined the Home Rule League in 1873 and fully supported the candidacy of Charles Stewart Parnell for Member of Parliament.

"What do you know of Parnell, Irishman," the British officer interrupted.

"Nothing but what I've read in the diary. James Connolly, that's another matter. I know a good bit about him . . . "

"Parnell, not Connolly is the question. I'm a student of Parnell's life," the officer remarked. He looked pensive and a bit melancholic.

"You, an Englishman, a student of Parnell?"

"Yes, and why not?"

Steven continued the story.

"Ya know, Teresa," Brian said while his sister rested in bed barely able to whisper with her congestion. "This fellow Parnell—he's a Protestant bloke from a wealthy family, but he puts me to mind of Wolfe Tone."

"Aye, but he's not as . . . militant . . . as Tone," Teresa rasped.

"He's for the separation of Ireland, or so he claims. He's our nation's answer to Kossuth or Mazzini."

"But we don't have a nation, Brian."

"Not yet we don't. I'm gona try to meet Mr. Parnell and tell him me thoughts about the matter. He's a head on the pole that I must communicate with. . . . "

"Ah whist about the pole dream or he'll think you to be crazy."

"I think I'll go to Wicklow for a talk with him."

"Do ya think he'll bother to listen?" Teresa rasped with a throaty voice.

"Indeed he will. He's a young man, ya know. Born about when I left for America. They say he's a powerful speaker in public though shy with individuals. So I don't think I'd be snubbed by the man at all. Besides with all me shaggy gray hair he'll think I'm a old grandfather or somethin', so he'll have to listen to me."

"Sure ya don't look *that* old."

"Aye, I've aged terrifically, Teresa. At forty-three I look, sixty-three. But . . . say, it's a grand day. Let me give you some air on the push chair today. It's glorious late summer weather with corncrakes hoppin' about and willy wagtails flyin' over the corn. Then I'll go out in the field and get us some spuds and cabbage for a fine supper."

"Sure, I'm too weak ta sit in any push chair today."

"I'll lift ya into it. Ya needn't worry."

He pushed her in the wheel chair along a country lane past hedgerows with blackberry vines and hawthorn bushes.

"Remember back in Cavan, Teresa. You and me would go pick blackberries before all that trouble."

"Aye," Teresa said glumly and began to weep. "Oh God, that dirty old Derid Joyce havin' us evicted! I wouldna' blame ya for shootin' the likes of him."

"Aye. Derid Joyce! At least Gladstone's Land Act is a step in the right direction. We need to have our three F's, fair rent, fixity of tenure, and free sale! It's a shame we cannot yet apply our rent to purchase. Our landlord is but another Derid Joyce."

"Aye, how many . . . farms . . . does that Englishman own?"

"Over thirty I s'pose. Of course he got them by bein' from gentry stock years back. But that's what I like about Parnell. He could easily be a landlord type, yet he's fightin' for a free Ireland!"

He pushed her up a brey to a spot not far from where Michael and Steven were being led by the British soldiers down to Fork Hill.

"Perhaps someday we'll have to fight for a free Ireland,"

Brian remarked.

"This Brian McBride," the British officer reflected, *"seemed like an interesting chap. I can understand his views. But blowing department stores in Belfast is no way to achieve a united Ireland."*

"What do ya expect after that '69 peace march ended in blood? Anyway, we've stopped blowin' up stores for the most part," Michael said. *"But we'll hit Parliament yet."*

"The hell ya will," snapped a soldier.

"Ya know, Teresa, it may even take fighting the British in *their* homeland. Wolfe Tone would have, as well as that brave lad called Robert Emmet."

"Aye," she rasped.

"I only wish me life would mean somethin' beyond what it is. I mean, here I am at forty-three and what have I done?"

"Written a diary."

"Sure who is gona read a bloody auld diary?"

"We've read it, haven't we Michael?"

"Aye!"

"Yes," the officer added. *"No man, I suppose does live in vain no matter what his views are. All this is sort of uncanny. Here we are talking about Brian and Teresa as though they were with us. It's as if Brian could pull a trigger and shoot us down through the century past.*

Brian pushed Teresa back home and made her a cup of tea to drink while he went out into the damp fields and dug a bucket of spuds and pulled a few heads of cabbage. Before too long he would have to dig a deep pit with his loy and push all of his fresh spuds in for winter storage. He would put a layer of clay, and a layer of reeds, and another layer of clay over them to keep them from frost of the approaching autumn. As he walked back up to his rented cottage with his Wellington boots all covered with clay, he waved to his sister sitting by the window sipping her tea. Black coal smoke rose in spirals from the grey chimney.

"Now we'll have a "mug-up" together once I put these spuds and cabbage in some boilin' water."

"Brian, will ya look at yer boots all covered with clay. Take them off would ya please!"

"Aye," Brian responded pensively and far off. "Ya know, after you went to bed last evenin' I went to our bookshelves by the fireplace to look for somethin' to read and settled for the Bible. I read in *Daniel* a passage about a shockin' great statue with feet of clay that crumbled when it was hit by a rolling rock from the mountainside. Here am I with me feet of clay! I hope Ireland isn't that part of the statue now."

"Ah, no, Brian. No more so . . . than any other nation. No more so . . . than the America you've told me about with its Mexican and Indian wars."

As the red sun sank over misty fields lined with chesnut trees, Brian brought in two plates of steaming spuds boiled in their jackets with salt and some cabbage covered with melted butter and pepper. The meal burnt their tongues, but they were hungry.

"Teresa, why did I ever leave ya? I shoulda' stayed in Dublin."

"To work in a brewery? What good would thata done ya? You're the better man fer havin' gone over there, Brian."

"Well, I wish I was as sure about it as you."

After several weeks of feverish work in his potato fields, Brian asked a neighbor's wife to care for Teresa while he went down to Wicklow by train to talk with Charles Stewart Parnell. But the M.P. was in London when he got there. He told the servants he'd wait around town until Parnell returned. There was a lovely patch of Irish woodlands nearby, as wild as Ireland must have been in prehistoric times when Celts were white Indians. Brian brushed past chest-high ferns growing in clusters under pine and hemlock. The undergrowth and leafy canopies above created darkness in the middle of the day as though the sun never existed. He walked up to one bright grassy knoll where sun rays peeped through the vegetation and stooped to pick some shamrocks and raspberries. If only he could speak to the honorable M.P. If only he could activate some of the historical principles he read about in his library back home. Ireland had to gain its independence and emerge as a communalistic agrarian nation. But the M.P. did not return to Wicklow after one week, and Brian left reluctantly for his County Down farm.

Horrible news awaited Brian upon his return. Teresa had died suddenly after being evicted for not being able to pay a higher rent demanded. The shock of eviction was too much for her, and she died in her neighbor's house while Brian was in Wicklow. The neighbor said she got a coughing fit that ended only with death. This event almost destroyed Brian who slept in rage out in the cold fields after his only loved one was buried in a Protestant cemetary below Slieve Gullion. He seemed crazed for a while confusing Teresa with Chilsipee. He wanted to catch her soul in an Indian gourd.

Brian walked back from the lonely graveyard a week later mumbling, "If only I hadn't spent those shillings on a meaningless railway ticket. I'm always leaving Teresa when she most needs me. What kind of crazy Irishman am I?"

He tramped over the muddy fields up to the chambered cairn several miles from his former farm with all those spuds going for higher rent. He worked the farm so hard to make it better that they raised the rent. All along he had the strange feeling they'd do just that. He hadn't worked so hard since his days back in French Canada. Perhaps he stored under the ground two or three thousand weight of potatoes, surely as many spuds in the ground as heads on the pole of his dreams.

"Where shall I go? The soup kitchens?"

"Michael," asked a British soldier, *"did he ever get to see Parnell?"*

"Aye. After he wandered around as a tramp and beggar on the verge of insanity. When was it? I think after Parnell had been jailed in Kilmainham. He apparently supported a 'No Rent Manifesto' while in jail as a counter-measure to unlordly landlords."

"Did this McBride chap talk to Parnell about his American experiences? Is that what inspired that manifesto? You said he did actually talk to him, didn't you?" asked the thoughtful British officer who had confiscated the diary and leafed through it back at the shed.

"Aye, Brian did that alright. Perhaps Parnell was reminded of old Brian Boru when he saw him. Anyway it was after the Kilmainham jailing that Brian saw Parnell."

"When was that, lad?"

"In the 1880's."

"I see."

"Well, anyway," Steven continued, "Brian got back his ancient job on Dublin-Cork Railway, and when was it now? I think the diary . . . oh, God! We left the diary back in the cowshed!"

"Little matter, maite. Ya got his life in yer head anyway."

"I think it was somewhere in the 1880's, maybe 1884 or 5 that he finally met Parnell. He had only five minutes with the M.P. but managed to talk of his Shoshone days and the evictions he had lived through. Perhaps Parnell thought him to be a bit touched, but he must have listened for it was in Cork . . . Brian left the clipping in the diary . . . that the Irish politician declared 'No man has a right to fix the boundary of the march of a nation; no man has a right to say to his country—this far shalt thou go and no further.'"

"You know, old chap," the officer remarked, "that might explain why such a parliamentarian as Parnell would have made such a brash statement. That speech of his in Cork wasn't like him if I've read my history correctly. He was caught between the radicals who wanted a violent revolution and the moderates who wanted home rule whereby Ireland would govern its internal but not external affairs."

"Aye," Michael retorted, "But it was a violent revolution that separated Ireland from England in the end, wasn't it?"

"Yes, Irishman, that it was. But why are you still fighting an old war that ended fifty years ago?"

The mist had cleared, and they all marched down a steep hill zigzagging above a bog where ancient bogmen digging up turf waved to all the gunmen.

"*We believe,*" Steven volunteered, "*that the 1921 partition created rather than solved problems. You can't have a divided nation with peace. Look at Viet Nam and Korea. Until puppet governments are overthrown and the country is reunited, there'll never be peace.*"

"*Truly, Irishman! But whatever became of Brian Mc-Bride?*" the officer questioned.

"*He was killed after he took back the farm in County Down by force. Brian mentions in his diary somethin' about a Wounded Knee massacre he read about in 1890. He said that this is one white Indian that wasn't going to be pushed around. Not old Brian Boru himself, no sir. Brian claimed his rights and lived there for a year or so until he was shot in the back while working out in the fields by his high and mighty landlord. I can just imagine the blood oozin' out of him while he slowly closed his eyes on the green fields of Ireland. It was the landlord, Mr. Mawton Jones, who had the nerve to write at the end of the McBride diary 'SHOT DEAD 1891 by yours truly.' The landlord must have left the musty auld book in a cowshed or the cowshed, I suppose, where you found us. But how he died is of little importance; it's how he lived that deserves our reflection.*"

Steven nodded to his comrade to look down at the chambered cairn. They spotted several black berets of the IRA hiding behind the mossy rocks. Steven spoke a few words in Gaelic to Michael saying at the count of three to run for it:

"*Aon, du, tri!*"

They bounded down the slopes as fast as they could toward the sacred chambered cairn built centuries before blue faced Britons ever knew where Ireland, EIRE, was. One of the British marksmen aimed his carbine at Steven and fired just as the IRA rebel lurched to the right. The hot bullet went through his shoulder as he and his buddy dove for cover at the cairn. Steven was smiling because he knew he hadn't been hit bad. Pain subsided to numbness.

"Bout time you blokes got back!" their friends shouted.

"Aye, indeed. We're gona have ta fill yous in on an old countryman by the name of Brian McBride," Michael panted.

"That'll have to wait, chaps. We got some mean business ta do first. But here's some grub fer yous while we try to give them boys some lead."

"Aye."

Steven and Michael ate ham sandwiches ravenously as the other eight rebels fired back at the tommies who fled toward the old cowshed. High velocity rifle fire flared back and forth till sunset echoing in the valley where a few compassionate farmers buried Brian's body years ago.

After Michael packed and dressed Steven's painful wound, the squad of merry rebels went down the slopes of Slieve Gullion in the darkness of midnight toward the twinkling lights of Newton-Hamilton and Crossmaglen. If Brian wasn't with Steven and Michael, he was certainly in them. They knew that this Ireland must be, for *all* Irishmen, free at last, free at last.

Envoi

A year after the British officer's encounter with the rebels on Slieve Gullion's slopes and his recovery from a nasty leg wound, he donated the confiscated McBride diary to his college library back in England. It became part of a manuscript collection of rebellious literature in which the school prided itself. Perhaps future scholars would attempt theoretical analyses. Meanwhile, an old round tower near Fork Hill got the name "McBride Tower." It became a regular meeting place for the outlawed Irish Republican Army and its sympathizers. Most of the jaw bone sessions held there concerned the formation of a new Ireland with four ancient provinces fully represented in Dublin at the

Dáil (Assembly): Ulster, Munster, Leinster, and Connacht; each province in turn would have its dáil, Ulster's being Dáil Uladh. Someday soon, they hoped to throw away their weapons and live in peace.

About the Author

Richard F. Fleck was born in Philadelphia in 1937 and went to Rutgers University where he graduated with honors in French literature and to the University of New Mexico where he received his Ph.D. in English. He has worked as a deck hand aboard a marine research vessel in the Delaware Bay, as a ranger for the National Park Service, as an assistant to the Rare Books Department of Princeton University Library, and is now Associate Professor of English at the University of Wyoming. In 1972-73 he took sabbatical leave in Ireland. His other books include *Palms, Peaks, and Prairies* (The Golden Quill Press, 1967), and *The Indians of Thoreau* (Hummingbird Press, 1974). His shorter literary pieces have appeared in numerous national journals including Victorian Poetry, Connecticut Review, Ariel, American Indian Quarterly, The Living Wilderness, International Poetry Review, Cthulhu Calls, and The Cape Rock Journal. This is Fleck's first novel.